TESLA'S SECRET PAPERS

KEEPING NIKOLA TESLA'S DREAM ALIVE

DAN SIZEMORE

TESLA'S SECRET PAPERS

*Keeping Nikola
Tesla's Dream Alive*

A Novel
By Dan Sizemore

"Electric power is everywhere present in unlimited quantities and can drive the world's machinery without the need for coal, oil or gas…"
– Nikola Tesla

TESLA'S SECRET PAPERS

A Science Fiction Thriller

Published 2017 by Dan Sizemore

www.dansizemore.com

Copyright ©2017 by Dan Sizemore

978-0-9855078-2-4 First Edition Paperback

978-0-9855078-3-1 e-book

1

The bullet grazed Jack's ear as he stepped off the bus. He grabbed his right ear and spun around to see if he could spot his attacker. Not suspecting his life would be in danger on a busy New York City street, Jack darted behind a newspaper stand, peering around the edge. Clutching a brown leather briefcase in his left hand, he placed his right hand up to his now throbbing ear. A stream of blood trickled down his index finger and dripped on his shoulder. His heart pounded out of his chest as his eyes darted around the street. A large group of people had gathered around a woman on the block behind Jack. Running towards them to lose himself in the crowd, Jack pushed his way in to get a closer look.

"Someone call 911!" yelled a man as he leaned over a woman's body on the ground. Jack could see that she had been shot in the face. Touching his bleeding ear, Jack said a quick silent prayer for the woman. Blood now trickled down half of his right hand as he held his ear.

"Dude, are you okay" asked a young man in a Yankees baseball cap standing beside him. Jack glanced at the blood on his hand, then turned to run down an alley and hide behind a large green dumpster covered with graffiti. Ambulance and police sirens filled the air as Jack stared out from behind the dumpster that smelled like something had died in it. His ear was beginning to burn, and he realized how close he had come to dying. If the bullet had hit an inch closer to his skull...

Jack inched his way from behind the dumpster away from the horrifying scene of the woman shot in the face. A gigantic rat scurried between his legs, startling him and almost causing him to trip. Sprinting through the alley to the next block he wondered if he'd hear a shot.

Traffic was stopped at the light as Jack exited the alley. Raising his now bloody briefcase in the air, Jack figured no taxi driver in New York would take on a passenger with a bloody right hand and ear, but a driver soon stopped for him.

"Where's the closest hospital? I've been shot," said Jack hopping in.

"Five blocks away. Geezus Christ, who shot you, man?" asked the old Hispanic driver as he looked in the mirror, grimacing at the blood running down Jack's hand from his ear.

"I'm not sure. I stepped off the bus and then the bullet hit me."

"Don't worry about the fare, buddy. It's on me," said the driver as he mashed on the gas, ran through a red light, narrowly missing a truck.

"I've always wanted to do that, ya know. Buckle up, man."

The driver swerved around traffic as Jack buckled his seat belt, leaving streaks of blood on the strap. Jack gripped the door with his bloody right hand while holding the briefcase up close against his chest. The next light was turning from yellow to red, and the cab engine roared as the driver raced to beat it. A businessman in a suit entered the crosswalk, looked up when he heard the revving engine, his mouth open wide. The man dove back onto the sidewalk while the cab driver veered to miss the pedestrian and slammed on his brakes to avoid another cab in the intersection. Jack braced himself and closed his eyes.

"Oh, shit..." yelled the cabbie as the tires screeched. The cab t-boned another yellow cab like a demolition derby. The force of the impact hurdled Jack forward causing the lap belt to crush his abdominal organs. He opened his eyes to see the other taxi driver emerge from his destroyed cab with a scowl on his face.

"You sonofabitch," screamed the Indian driver. "Didn't you see the red light?"

"I was taking a man to the hospital," yelled Jack's driver as he stuck his head out of the window. "He was shot in the head, man."

Jack had to push on his door with his shoulder several times to emerge from the back seat. Steam poured from the front of the cab and broken glass crunched under his feet. Jack spotted the hospital a block away and limped across the intersection trying to avoid stepping on more glass.

"Hey, no charge for the ride, man," yelled the cabbie in Jack's direction as he headed straight for the hospital without looking back. His knees ached from the collision, but at least it took his attention away from the pain in his ear. He could hear the cab drivers continue to yell at each other as he hobbled down the block still clutching his briefcase.

Walking into the emergency room entrance, Jack saw a packed room with several people sprawled on the floor including a man who sat in the corner with his head in his hands. Jack smeared some blood over his face from his right hand and exaggerated his limp as he approached the receptionist.

"I was robbed and got in a car accident on the way here."

The receptionist eyed Jack carefully noting his bloody face. "Name please."

"Jack Cullen."

"Drivers license and insurance card. I'll fill out the forms since you'll just bleed all over them," she said impatiently. "Nurse, get Mr. Cullen a room *stat*."

A young blonde nurse came out and led Jack to a bed with a curtain around it as doctors and nurses scurried around. She took his blood pressure and gave him some gauze to place over his wound. After a few minutes, a different nurse entered.

"So, were you shot anywhere other than your ear?" asked the new nurse.

"No. But I was also in a car accident on the way here. My knees are pretty banged up."

"Let's have a look at that ear. You can place the briefcase on the floor." Jack set the briefcase down and rested his feet on top of it.

"What do you have in there, money?" she asked as she cleaned up his ear wound and wiped the blood off his face. Jack grimaced as she worked on his ear.

"Nothing, really."

"Uh-huh. You'll need a couple of stitches in your ear lobe and you'll be just fine. Let's have a look at those knees."

Jack rolled up his pants legs with his right hand as he kept one foot on the briefcase.

"Here, let me help you with that," said the nurse bending down to help him. "They just look bruised. Can you get up and walk for me?"

"Sure," said Jack as he slid off the treatment table and limped across the room keeping an eye on his briefcase.

"You couldn't do that with broken kneecaps. If you want, you can wait a while for some x-rays of those knees. We're pretty swamped, so others with more serious injuries will come first."

"I think I'll be okay. Just fix up my ear and I'll be on my way."

"You'll just have to sign some discharge papers saying you refused an x-ray. This won't take long," she said as she grabbed her needle to numb his ear, causing him to grimace.

"The numbing is worse than the stitches," said the nurse as she began to stitch him up. "Were you the victim of a robbery?"

"Yes. Another lady got shot in the face."

"Oh, we've got her in here now. She's in pretty bad shape. You were lucky."

"I guess so." Jack winced as she finished stitching his ear.

"Just leave these in for a week and have your doctor remove them."

"Thanks," said Jack as he slipped off the

examination table and picked up his briefcase. Jack left the room and could feel the nurses' eyes following him down the hall. He turned around to look at her as she placed a call on her cell phone. Glancing at his reflection in a glass door, Jack saw the white bandage on his right ear. As he stepped onto the busy sidewalk outside the emergency room, another ambulance pulled up with its sirens blaring. Jack walked down the block and checked all around him before ducking into a Starbucks on the corner. The place was bustling with customers, and he spotted an empty table in the back.

He sat down against the wall, placing the leather briefcase on the table. Glancing around nervously, he unsnapped the latch and opened the briefcase. A thick file folder was stuffed with papers and had the words "Tesla Papers" written in ink on the tab. The papers in the two-inch thick stack were yellowed and tattered around the edges. Jack pulled two large red rubber bands off the file as he looked around him again. The first page was filled with neat handwriting Jack recognized immediately. His hands shook as he scanned the first page that he knew was in the original handwriting of the mystical electrical genius himself. The U.S. government had confiscated Tesla's papers from his apartment after his death to keep his advanced weaponry ideas out of the hands of its enemies. There were, however, stories that Tesla gave away some of his papers to pay off his debts.

Could these papers be from Tesla's hotel debt repayment? thought Jack as he started to read.

Ever since I brought forth the AC induction motor, my mind has been working out the details of my next invention to change the world. I see these visions clearly in my mind and know that they will work. There is no need to draw a schematic since I work all the problems out in my mind. After the successful introduction of AC current from Niagara Falls to the city of Buffalo, I have been able to acquire financial backing from some of the most well-known businessmen in New York. They have been quite astounded at what I have told them I plan to do. In fact, most of them believe I am some sort of a mad scientist. They cling to their present beliefs and their money, but I know the future is mine.

Jack turned the fragile page so quickly he almost tore it in half. Sensing that someone was watching him, he looked up to see three dark skinned men in black suits with sunglasses crossing the street, and his heartbeat quickened. The papers related to Tesla on Craigslist had generated many curious but strange inquirers.

Jack shut the briefcase and stood up from the table while keeping his eyes on the men as he headed towards the rear exit. He darted out and stood with his back against an outside wall trying to figure out what to do next. His heart felt like it was going to explode, but he just needed a quiet place to sit down alone and finish reading the papers. The men after him must have contacted the woman he bought the box of papers from yesterday. Her life was in danger, and he had to warn her if she wasn't dead already.

Just then the three men in black suits came around the corner of the building, and Jack froze, not knowing where to run. The men were no more than fifty feet away, approaching Jack slowly. He glanced to his left, and to his amazement a middle-aged black police officer stood beside his patrol car writing a parking ticket. Jack sprinted towards the police car as one of the men pulled out a pistol and fired at him. The bullet whizzed past Jack's head and shattered the rear view mirror of the police car.

Wayne Claiborne had been a police officer for twenty years, but this was the first time he had ever been shot at. He looked up to see a crazed man with a briefcase running straight at him.

"Help!" screamed Jack as he rushed towards the car door. Wayne reached over and opened the door as Jack piled in. Another bullet pierced the rear window as Wayne got in and mashed the accelerator.

"Who are they and why are they shooting at you," yelled the officer.

"I don't know."

"Adam Twelve, code eight," Wayne shouted into his radio as he barreled down the street.

"Twelve, code eight, go ahead," replied the dispatcher.

"Shots fired outside 81st and Broadway Starbucks. Suspects are three dark skinned males in dark suits."

"Affirmative. Backup is being called."

"I'm code four for now," said Wayne.

"Copy Twelve."

"Okay, was this a drug deal gone bad?" Officer Claiborne asked Jack.

"Just get me away from them!"

"Listen, I gotta do my job, dammit. You could be a witness to a crime. Stay here while I go back for those guys."

Officer Claiborne parked his car two blocks away and got out with his gun drawn as Jack peered out of the back window.

"Keep your head down, dammit!" said the officer. Within minutes two more police cars pulled in front of the Starbucks with their lights flashing and sirens blaring. Two officers from each car emerged and approached Officer Claiborne.

"No suspects here. Check with someone inside to see if they spotted them," said one officer. The second cop entered Starbucks and questioned several customers while the other two officers crossed the street on foot. After several minutes, all of the cops met outside with Officer Claiborne.

"Several people reported seeing three men in suits and they heard gunshots, but no one saw where they went," said one of the cops.

"We fanned out over several blocks and didn't see em'," said the second officer.

"How could three guys in dark suits and sunglasses fire two shots in broad daylight and then disappear?" asked Officer Claiborne throwing his hands in the air. "Those guys blew out my mirror and my rear windshield, and I've got a witness back there in my car. I'll get a statement from him while you guys keep looking. Maybe we can pull a bullet outta my car," he said as he walked back to find Jack slouched in the back seat.

"Okay, I'm gonna have to ask you some questions," said Claiborne as he got in and started the car. "What's your name?"

"Jack."

"Jack what?"

"Jack Cullen."

"Why did those men fire at you?"

"I don't know."

"You got drugs in that briefcase?"

"No, and even if I did, I woulda pitched them by now."

"True. Whatchu got there? You got some kinda death grip on it."

"Just a bunch of old papers."

"Well, we'll just have a look at them in a minute."

"I don't think that's such a good idea."

"Why not? You got somethin' to hide?"

"I'm not sure of what's in there. I just got to look at them briefly."

"Listen, I almost got killed today by somebody shootin' at you. So you must have something they really want. You can tell me now or I can arrest you."

Jack hesitated for a few seconds before answering.

"Okay, if you pull over I'll let you see what's in the briefcase. I don't want everyone in your station sticking their nose in this. This is extremely sensitive stuff, so I'll have to ask you for your complete confidence."

"You know I can't do that. If you've got stolen property in there, it's a crime."

"It's not stolen. I paid for these papers."

Officer Claiborne had now pulled over to the side of the road.

"What kinda papers?" asked the officer.

"Have you ever heard of the scientist Nikola Tesla?"

"Who?"

"Nikola Tesla invented the AC induction motor, wireless communication, remote control, robotics, and hundreds of other patents. He was a visionary who made bold predictions to the world about his discoveries. A hundred years ago he claimed to receive communications from other planets, and he talked about death rays shooting planes out of the sky in the 1930's. He offered his ideas to the U.S. government before WWII, but they didn't listen. When he died penniless in his New York apartment in 1943, the FBI came and took all his papers...truckloads of em'. To this day their contents have remained classified."

"So, you got some of those top secret papers in that briefcase?"

"No, but I've got other papers he wrote that the government knows nothing about. You see, Tesla constantly had money problems and moved from hotel to hotel in New York for years. To pay his outstanding hotel bill, he would simply turn over some of his papers to the hotel. Well, I've got some of those in here," Jack said pointing to his briefcase.

"Well, let's take a look at em.'"

"Officer...Claiborne," said Jack looking at his name tag, "Before I do that, I'm afraid I'm going to ask for your help."

"What kinda help is that?"

"I bet the people that shot at me know where I live, and I'm in danger if I go back there. In fact, I'll probably have to move out of the country. This information needs to get out to the world. That's what Tesla wanted, and I'm going to be the guy that reveals his secrets."

"Don't look at me. Hell, I just met you. I ain't no secret service."

"You know people, though." Jack looked around and turned his gaze back to his briefcase. "I'm dying to know what's in here," he said as he popped open the locks on the briefcase. Officer Claiborne placed his hand on his holster and leaned over to get a closer look. Jack pulled out the musty papers again and removed the rubber bands so not to tear the paper.

"Where did you get these papers?" asked Claiborne.

"Would you believe they were listed on Craigslist? A lady listed some old scientific papers for sale she had found in her basement, and I contacted her immediately. Her grandfather had managed the Hotel St. Regis where Tesla used to live. Tesla sold the papers to the hotel to pay off his bill, and her grandfather brought them home from work. He set them aside and forgot about em', and her father inherited them. He could have thrown them away never realizing what he had. Her dad died recently, and she posted an ad to sell some old scientific papers from someone named Tesla for twenty-five dollars. I offered her twenty, and she took it."

"Wow, you lucked out. Why were you so interested in this in the first place?"

"I'm an electrical engineer, and I first learned about Tesla in college. I did some more research on him and became fascinated with his life. I think most of his findings are secretly held at Wright-Patterson Air Force Base."

"Well, let's take a look," said Wayne. Jack flipped through the papers to where he had left off.

I have contemplated the problem of delivering energy freely throughout the world, particularly after the destruction of my wireless transmitting tower. I am quite certain that an abundant supply of free electricity is available to every person on the planet. Energy is all around us, but man has not understood how to tap into it yet. I have formulated a simple device for the transmission of an unlimited supply of free energy everywhere. This device can be hooked up to any home or business to provide all of its power needs. I have not tested this device with a working model, but after my experiments in Colorado Springs in 1899, I am convinced of the inevitability of its success. There are those who stand to lose financially from the introduction of this device, but the progress of mankind cannot afford the withholding of this discovery for the pure sake of lost profits. I have enlisted the help of a technical designer to draw an exact replica with the dimensions I have formulated in my mind. The next several pages show the design and materials needed to construct this device.

"Is this for real, 'cause I want in on this action," said Officer Claiborne. "My electric bill was over $400 last month. I'll take free any day."

"This is why I'm being pursued," said Jack pointing to the drawings. "Somebody doesn't want this information out, and those guys with suits are part of it. The lady that sold me this is in great danger. I need to warn her right away."

Jack pulled out his cell to look up her number. Officer Claiborne noticed Jack's fingers shaking as he searched his contact list on his phone.

"Who would want to keep this a secret?" asked the officer.

"Lots of people. The utility companies. OPEC. The natural gas industry is exploding, and they're counting on tapping into the huge reservoirs of natural gas in the U.S. If this comes out, they're outta business."

Jack found the seller's number and dialed it. After a few rings the call went to voicemail.

"Ginny, this is Jack Cullen, the guy who bought your old papers. Listen, there's something important I need to tell you about the papers you sold me. Call me back as soon as you can."

"Officer, I'm asking you again to please help me find a place to stay. My life is in danger, and I can't go back to my home. Fortunately, my son is away at college, and I'm divorced, so no one is home."

"I can't believe I'm even considering this, but I'll let you stay for a week. That's it. Man, my wife is gonna kill me."

"Thanks, Officer. I really appreciate it. We can take another look at these schematics tonight. Who knows, maybe we'll sell this information to the world and get rich."

"Now you're talkin'. Fifty-fifty, right?"

"Sure. Just get me outta here, Officer."

"You can call me Wayne. I have to stop by the station first to file a report. It shouldn't take long. The two partners shook hands, and Wayne took off in the traffic towards the station. As they turned the corner onto Broadway, a man in a suit behind a dumpster in an alley took a picture of Officer Wayne Claiborne's passing patrol car.

2

Betty Claiborne was getting an after school snack ready for her two young children when she saw her husband's bullet ridden police car pull into their driveway. As the garage door opened, Betty was surprised to see someone she didn't know in the front seat with her husband and went out to meet them.

"What happened to your car? Why didn't you call me?" asked Betty as she eyed the stranger getting out of the car.

"Honey, I'm sorry I didn't call you. I'm okay, just some crazy people out there. This is Jack Cullen. Jack, this is my wife, Betty."

"Hello, nice to meet you," said Jack as he reached to shake her hand.

"Jack's gonna have dinner with us tonight, if that's okay."

"Sure," said Betty not knowing what else to say.

"May I use your restroom?" asked Jack.

"Yes, it's the first door on the right in the hallway," said Betty.

"Thanks." Jack entered the house, leaving Betty and Wayne behind.

"So, who's this guy? He's not a drug dealer, is he?"

"No, not at all. He just got into a little jam and needed some help."

"So, you invite a total stranger to dinner without even asking me. I don't mind feeding someone, but I gotta know in advance so I can prepare for it."

"I'm sorry. I know I shoulda called. But he needs help."

"What's his story? Is he in a nasty divorce?"

"No, well...he actually needs a place to stay for a few nights. But no more than a week."

"What!? You promised a stranger he could stay in our house for a week? Are you crazy? Why does he need a place to stay?"

"Somebody tried to shoot him today, and he's afraid to go home."

"Are you insane?" asked Betty. "So you come home with bullet holes in your car and invite a stranger somebody is trying to kill into our home for a week.

Did you remember that we've got two little kids at home?"

"Honey, we'll be just fine. Those guys will never find him here."

"Oh, this gets better. So, how many guys are after him?"

"Uh,...three. I think."

"That's just great. Why don't you just have him get a hotel room?"

"I'm sure he will soon. But for now he needs protection."

"Protection? Who's gonna protect us?"

"Me."

"I don't believe this. How could you?"

Inside, Jack could hear them arguing and wondered if he should tell her about the information he had in his briefcase to help her understand. Betty and Wayne stepped into the kitchen from the garage looking like they each had swallowed a lemon.

"Listen, I know this is awkward. You don't know me, and you've got kids here. I'll just go find a hotel somewhere," said Jack.

A look of relief spread across Wayne's face. "Okay, why don't we work on that tomorrow. But, tonight you can stay here. I did promise you that. Is that okay with you, honey?"

Betty hesitated before answering. "That's fine. I'll

get started on dinner," she said as she turned towards the kitchen. Wayne gestured for Jack to follow him into the dining room. Family pictures lined the wall above an antique mahogany sideboard. Jack set his briefcase on the table as they sat down.

"I'm sorry for putting you on the spot like this. Thanks for letting me stay tonight. I know she's not happy about this."

"It's okay. She'll fuss some, but she's great," said Wayne. "How 'bout we take a look at those papers again. I wanna know more about this Tesla guy. I'd never heard of him before."

"He was an amazing innovator who was so far ahead of his time that people couldn't comprehend his ideas. He was more interested in his work and the betterment of mankind than making a personal fortune."

"Speaking of fortunes, why don't we read some more about this idea of free electricity for everyone. I'm all over that."

"Yeah. I've googled this idea of a device for free electricity before, but I was never sure if it worked." Jack opened up the papers to the schematic drawings Tesla referred to and scanned them.

"This is cool. See how the magnets with coils turn the motor. Then two metal grounded Tesla coils are stuck into the ground. This is not too complicated, it seems."

"How does this thing create energy, though?" asked Wayne.

"It doesn't really create energy. It just draws the electrical potential that exists already in the ground and in the air. Tesla believed the earth was one big electrical ball of energy. All he had to do was find some way to harness it."

"How come nobody else has done this yet?"

"Because nobody else has seen this schematic before. Only Tesla could have come up with this! That's why they're trying to kill me. This information would change the world, and too many people stand to lose big time."

"Could we build one of these?"

"Maybe. Tesla didn't construct all of his inventions. He had it all in his head and would just tell an engineer the specifications he wanted."

"I've got a buddy that has a Master's degree in electrical engineering. You want me to call him?"

"No, I don't want to get anyone else involved yet. There is too much danger. I'll just keep reading on here and see if we could do it on our own."

Betty came in with her arms around her kids to introduce them to their dinner guest.

"Kids, this is Mr. Cullen. He will be having dinner with us tonight. These are our children Derrick and Sabrina."

"Hello. And how old are you?" asked Jack as he looked at Derrick.

"I'm nine. My sister is seven."

"Nice to meet you." Betty turned them back around and marched them into the kitchen.

"Did Daddy arrest him?" asked Derrick.

"Yes, he did. But it wasn't anything too bad. He'll be leaving tomorrow."

"But he doesn't have any handcuffs on. Why is that?"

"I think Daddy trusts him. Now you two go watch television until dinner is ready. I don't want you playing outside today," said Betty as she peered out of the window. Wayne left Jack alone to go help Betty with dinner.

Jack spent another hour reading the Tesla papers. Most of the pages were technical explanations of the schematics, but the last paragraph caught his attention.

I know it is imperative that this information is given to the world in the right way at the right time. The forces against free electricity for all are too strong to introduce now. This information must not die with me. I have given a copy of these plans to one other person, and he has been instructed to pass it down to one person in each generation until the time is ready to give it to the world.

Mr. Astor hired an extraordinary man to manage the hotel, and he is the other recipient of this priceless document. His name is Vincent Royal.

My purpose in life is to improve the condition of mankind. My mind never stops thinking of ways to ease the burdensome toils of everyday life. Brilliant flashes of light fill my dreams causing me much discomfort, but I can rest in peace knowing that my ideas have elevated the state of my fellow man.

Nikola Tesla, Oct. 22, 1918

Jack stared in disbelief at what he had just read, so he reread the paragraph. Was there a living descendant of someone named Vincent Royal that had access to these papers? And who was this Mr. Astor? Jack pulled out his cell phone and googled the history of the St. Regis Hotel in New York. He discovered that the man named Astor was most likely the famous millionaire John Jacob Astor who founded the hotel. Jack read that the St. Regis was built in 1904, and John Jacob Astor perished on the Titanic disaster eight years later. *Good thing Tesla didn't give Astor this document,* thought Jack.

"Jack, you wanna get washed up for dinner?" asked Wayne from the kitchen.

"Sure thing. You should read some of this Tesla history."

"Like what?" asked Wayne.

"He worked for Thomas Edison but had a falling out with him. There was a huge battle between the two eventually over alternating versus direct current. Tesla won with alternating current which we still use today," said Jack.

"I never learned anything about Tesla in school," said Wayne.

"Not many people did. Makes we wonder if it was an intentional omission."

"Come get washed up for dinner," said Wayne as they headed towards the kitchen.

"I forgot to ask you if you like chicken and mashed potatoes," said Betty.

"Oh, of course I do. This looks great."

"Derrick, would you like to say grace?" asked Betty.

"Uh, okay." Derrick placed his hands in prayer under his chin and closed his eyes.

"Dear Jesus, thank you for all my baseball friends and my Coach Stewart. Thank you for all this food, and try to keep our guest tonight outta jail. Momma says that Daddy trusts him so he can't be all bad. Amen."

A moment of awkward silence filled the kitchen.

"Honey, nobody said Mr. Cullen was going to jail," said Betty.

"You said Daddy arrested him."

"You told him that?" asked Wayne.

"No, I just said he was in some trouble."

"It's okay," said Jack to Derrick. "I'm not going to jail."

"That's right," added Wayne. "In fact, Jack and I are gonna be business partners together. Right Jack?"

"Absolutely. As long as we can find a buyer."

"Buyer for what?" asked Betty as she filled Sabrina's plate with mashed potatoes.

"I've gotten hold of some information that could allow anyone to get electricity free from wherever they live. No more power lines or electric bills. If it really works, it will revolutionize the world. I just have to make a working prototype," said Jack.

Betty stared a deadpan look at Jack and then Wayne.

"You believe this stuff?" asked Betty looking at her husband.

"Well, it sounds great from what Jack has said. He's agreed to go fifty-fifty with me, and I've got no skin in the game, so if it doesn't pan out, I haven't lost anything. So all it has is upside potential."

"And you're willing to put your family in danger based on some pipe dream written on some old papers?"

"Are we in danger, Mommy?" asked Derrick.

"No, No. I was just kidding," said Betty.

"Honey, I..." said Wayne as he thought he saw something out the window in his back yard. It was beginning to get dark, so Wayne got up to get a closer look, grabbing his gun as a matter of habit.

"Don't worry, honey. I'm just gonna go check this out."

Peering out of the window by his kitchen sink, Wayne saw nothing and opened the back door to listen. Standing on his back porch, he scanned the yard and back woods for movement, but everything was quiet in his suburban neighborhood. A beautiful lone dove landed on his birdfeeder, and Wayne was taken aback since he had never seen a dove in his yard before. After a minute or so, he came back in and locked the door.

"Coast is clear," he said in a reassuring tone. Just then his doorbell rang, and Wayne walked to his front door. He peered through the peephole in his solid oak door and saw a Middle Eastern man in a dark suit and sunglasses standing on his front porch. Wayne stepped away from the door, his heart racing. He had been looking in his mirror all the way home and was sure no one was following him.

"Who was it?" asked Betty as she took a bite of chicken.

"We need to leave now. One of the men who shot at us today is at the front door. Let's get into the car and go. There could be three of them, and I can't fend off all three."

"Can't you call 911?" asked Betty.

"I'd probably get fired for trying to hide a witness in my home. We don't have time."

Derrick and Sabrina both started crying.

"Hush, children. I need both of you to be quiet right now. Let's do like Daddy said and get into the car right now."

"Can I bring my blankie?" asked Sabrina.

"Only if it's downstairs. Oh, I see it on the couch. Go get it darling."

"I'll grab my papers from the dining room," said Jack as he jumped up from the table. From the dining room Jack could see the man in the dark suit standing on the front porch. Another man was parked in a car on the street in front of the house. *Where is the third guy?* thought Jack as he grabbed the Tesla papers and rushed into the garage to join the others.

"Betty, you drive while I'll be in the front seat with my gun. The rest of you huddle down in the back and keep your heads down. Everything's gonna be all right," said Wayne as he tried to display a façade of calmness. Betty took her seat behind the wheel while Wayne took his gun off safety.

"Are you ready for this?" asked Wayne.

"Let's do it," said Betty as she started the engine of his police car. Wayne touched the garage door opener, and the door slowly began to open. Betty looked out of her rear view mirror and wished the car was parked heading out so she wouldn't have to back out. As the door got halfway up, Betty caught sight of a man's legs standing in the driveway behind her. As the door fully opened, Wayne saw a man in a black suit and sunglasses drawing a gun out from his jacket.

"Mash it!" yelled Wayne with his gun drawn. Betty floored the accelerator and watched the man behind her raise his gun up. In an instant the police car smashed into the man before he could fire. Jack crouched low in the back seat and heard a sickening thud sound as the car barreled into the armed man. Betty saw him disappear from view in her rear view mirror as she stomped on her brakes and turned her wheels to leave the driveway. As Betty frantically put the car in drive, Wayne saw the man on the front porch come racing around the corner.

The man who was run over had become tangled and caught underneath the police car. A trail of blood streaked down the driveway as Betty picked up speed. As the car hit the entrance to the street, Betty was doing 35 mph, and the car bounced up in the air dislodging the crumpled body from underneath the car. A man parked in the waiting car on the street got out to check on his partner lying in a heap on the road. His mangled body lay in a pool of blood on the asphalt, and the first assailant from the front door helped lift him up and put his lifeless bloody body in the back seat.

"Are they behind us?" yelled Betty as they careened onto the ramp to the interstate.

"I haven't seen anybody following us," said Wayne as he craned his neck looking behind him.

"Can we sit up now?" asked Jack. "I thought I was going to throw up the way Betty was driving. Good lord, were you a race car driver in a previous life?"

"I gotta do whatever I can to protect my family," said Betty.

"Nice job honey," said Wayne smiling at her.

"What the hell are we gonna do now?" asked Betty. Those guys aren't gonna quit looking for us. Where do we stay? I hope you got some answers. And we ain't staying with my sister. Last thing I wanna do is put my family in danger."

"I guess I'll have to call my boss and see if we can stay with him," said Wayne.

"What do we do with your good luck charm friend back there? Is your boss gonna want a stranger in his house with people trying to kill him?"

Wayne looked straight ahead thinking of what to do.

"I'll be okay," said Jack. "I've put enough people in danger already. I'm sorry for what I've gotten you into.

"There's a Marriott at the next exit. Is that okay with you," asked Betty.

"Sure," said Jack.

"Sounds like you're a little too eager to get rid of

him," said Wayne. "Why don't we just pull up to the Marriott and push him out of the car while we're rollin' through the parking lot."

"He's a grown man. Look what he's gotten us into today. I'm afraid to stay in my own house now. Do you have any better suggestions?" asked Betty.

"I'm sorry, Jack. Looks like this is the end of the line. Here's my card if you need somethin'. I can't put you up, but I can still help you. Are you gonna be okay?"

"Yeah, I'll be fine," said Jack as he opened the back door.

"Daddy, do you always let people go that you've arrested?" asked Derrick.

"Son, I didn't arrest him. I was just trying to help him out."

Jack stood in the parking lot with his briefcase and bandaged ear and leaned over to shake Wayne's hand. "Maybe under different circumstances we could have been friends. I appreciate your help. I'm sorry I put your family through all this."

"It's okay," said Wayne as he got out of the car. "Betty, I'll drive now."

"Fifty-fifty, right?" said Wayne as he reached out to shake Jack's hand, once again.

"Sure. As long as I'm still alive."

"I think you're gonna be all right. Call me. Okay?"

Wayne got in the police car and pulled away.

Sabrina and Derrick waved from the back window as they pulled out of the Marriott parking lot. Jack stood alone with his briefcase and waved goodbye, then checked into the Marriott and retreated to his room to read more of his Tesla papers. He peered out from a slit in the curtains of his room before plopping down on his bed to see if free electricity was real. At least now there were only two after him.

3

Jack awoke the next morning in the same clothes he wore the day before, but returning to his home to get more clothes was out of the question now. He was worried that he hadn't heard back from the woman who had sold him the Tesla papers and wanted to warn her that she was in danger.

Jack walked a mile to a rental car agency and drove out of the parking lot in a sporty white Ford Mustang. Driving past a Wal-Mart, he pulled in and picked up some spare clothes and toiletries. When he walked out of the Wal-Mart in jeans, t-shirt, dark sunglasses, and running shoes, he plugged in the address of the woman he bought the papers from on his phone GPS and headed back to New York.

After an hour drive, Jack found the apartment

building in Manhattan. He drove around the block several times to see if anyone was watching the building. Parking his car, he called her cell number again and got another voice mail recording. The front door of the building opened, and he recognized the same two Middle-Eastern men in dark suits that had shot at him. Jack sunk low in his seat and watched the men walk down the steps and enter a car. He heaved a sigh of relief as the two men pulled away into traffic.

Jack opened his briefcase to read the Tesla papers again, and flipping past the drawings of the free energy device, he spotted a hand drawing of a strange looking tower on the back of one of the pages. The tower had a large circular top that resembled a huge globe, and underneath was written the word Wardenclyffe. Jack knew Wardenclyffe was Tesla's grand project for the worldwide broadcasting and transmission of wireless electricity. The main financier of the project was J.P. Morgan, but he pulled the plug on funding after learning that Tesla had plans to give away free electricity. The tower was torn down before completion, but the laboratory Tesla worked out of was still standing on the site on Long Island. The old tower was rumored to have a vast honeycomb of underground tunnels.

A loud police siren interrupted Jack's train of thought, and he looked up to see two police cars pull up to the apartment building. Two officers emerged from each car and charged up the steps to the building. An ambulance pulled up behind, and two paramedics entered the building with the police officers. After about ten minutes, the paramedics came out with a body covered in a sheet on a stretcher.

Jack decided it was time to go immediately to Wardenclyffe for some answers, so he input the address in his GPS and headed to Long Island. He stopped by a hardware store to buy a flashlight and some wire cutters since he had suspected a fence surrounded Wardenclyffe, waiting until just before dusk to leave. Traffic was heavy, but Jack smiled when he saw a sign that said *Tesla Street,* and the red brick laboratory building that Tesla had built came into view. Sure enough, a chain link fence surrounded the property with No Trespassing signs posted everywhere. The huge headquarters of the Agfa Corporation loomed next door, so Jack pulled well off the road, turned off his lights and locked his briefcase in the trunk.

The night air was brisk as Jack walked to the rear fence surrounding the laboratory and knelt down with his wire cutters. He cut a small opening in the bottom of the fence and belly crawled underneath it. A near full moon made it unnecessary to use his flashlight as he approached the lab. All of the windows had been boarded up, but around back he found one board had been pried away from a window. There was just enough room to slip in, and Jack pulled himself up and wriggled through the opening. His feet hit shattered glass on the concrete floor, and the crunchy sound echoed through the empty dark room. His hands shook as he pulled out his flashlight and took a look around.

The light revealed a large room barren of furniture with large spider webs in each corner and broken glass scattered over the floor beneath the boarded windows. A chill went up Jack's spine as he imagined the great Tesla working through the night in the very room he was in. He exited the room and walked down the dark hall to a larger empty room when a mouse scurried across his path as he stood in the middle of the room dead still. Taking a deep breath, he imagined Tesla testing some of his incredible electrical experiments at one of the lab tables left behind. Tesla wore stylish suits and white gloves when at work and struck an imposing figure with his thin 6' foot 6" frame. Some even speculated that his ideas were so advanced that he was not of this world.

"What do you want from me, Tesla?" Jack said out loud. "You still have secrets that the world needs to know. Reveal them to me. I can help your spirit rest in peace." Jack heard his words reverberate against the barren walls and floors, and a cold chill blew across his face. Startled, Jack cast his flashlight in the direction of the boarded windows thinking a breeze had blown in from a broken pane. There was no broken window that he could see, but a voice came from behind him causing him to turn around and flash his light to see who was in the room with him. No one was there, but he was sure that he had heard a voice. Jack stood still and listened for it again. After a few seconds, the unmistakable sound of a male voice echoed from the walls, this time a bit louder.

"Three in the ground," the voice said.

Jack stood stunned not knowing if he was hearing voices in his head.

"Did you say three in the ground?" asked Jack aloud. Ten long seconds later he heard it again.

"Three in the ground," said the voice.

"Is that you, Tesla?" whispered Jack, his voice quivering. "What does that mean?"

He felt another strong rush of cold air hit him blowing back his hair as if a ghost had come and gone. *Was Tesla was trying to tell me something? Three of what in the ground? Three dead people?* Jack pondered the answer as he stumbled out of the room and down the hallway back to where he entered. If the answer was in the ground, then he would find nothing in a lab with concrete floors. He decided he had to go back outside to continue his search. Jack found the window he had entered and pushed himself up on the sill. As he hung there, he prayed nothing or no one would grab his ankles. He had always thought ghost stories were for crackpots, but now he wasn't so sure as he squeezed through the window and fell hands first onto the ground. Jumping up, Jack wandered to the grassy area behind the lab where Tesla's huge communication tower once stood. Concrete slabs still remained at the base of the tower which had been destroyed with explosives at the advent of WWI. Jack stood on a slab and gazed up into the starry sky imagining how magnificent the tower must have looked in its day. *The world was not ready for you, Tesla,* thought Jack.

Jack walked the perimeter of the tower base to get a feel of how massive it had been. He had read that the supporting beams in the ground were buried just as deep in the ground as the tower was high. Tesla made sure his tower was very well grounded to tap into the earth's energy. There had been heavy rainstorms earlier in the day, and Jack slipped on a muddy spot, falling on his side. As he got up and took a step forward, the ground beneath him suddenly gave way. Jack felt himself falling deep into the ground with muddy mounds of dirt cascading all around him. He tried grasping upwards with his hands, but there was nothing to grab onto. He braced himself, terrified that he would be buried alive in a hellish sinkhole. Jack struck the side of the hole and fell several feet sideways. Reaching out, he felt a ledge and pulled himself up into an opening, causing dirt and mud to splash into water far below. He was now enveloped in absolute darkness in an opening about four feet wide, and he found his flashlight somehow still in his pants pocket. Jack pulled it out and shined the light around him revealing a gaping sinkhole with mud still falling down into a mud pit far below. The only light came from the near full moon in the night sky.

Jack knew there was no way up out of the sinkhole as he was at least 50 feet underground with no rope. His only chance was to crawl through the shaft to find another way out, so Jack began his slow crawl and prayed its thin walls would not cave in on him. He could tell the shaft was man-made with its smooth walls. After slogging through the muck for about 20 feet, his flashlight shone on something bright ahead. Jack wiped the mud away from his eyes and squinted at the strong reflection of something shiny. He inched forward on his belly with his flashlight guiding him towards the object. As Jack got within a few feet, he recognized the object was a large safe. *Who in the hell would put a safe so far underground? Tesla! It had to be him. This was where he would bury his secrets! How fitting that they be buried under his tower.*

Jack scrambled up to the safe and noticed how it was sitting on a small slab of concrete. He gave it a few raps beside a large round combination knob on the left side of the door. Jack turned the combination knob feeling how smoothly it moved, even after 100 years. He could spend an eternity guessing the combination, but he knew he had to try to enter the safe now. Jack put his head in his hands and wracked his brain for some possible combinations Tesla would have used. He knew his birthday, so he tried that to no avail. What numbers had significance for Tesla? Then Jack remembered the voice he heard earlier that said three in the ground. That's it! Tesla had a fondness for the number three and anything divisible by three.

Jack started spinning the dial right, left, and then right to the numbers three, six and nine. *Too easy*, he thought. Jack continued with different multiples starting with the number three, and after an hour of unsuccessful attempts he took a break. His back stiffened up as he realized he must have hit it hard as he bounced onto the ledge in the sinkhole. *Even if I am able to open the safe, how am I going to get out of this hole?* Jack put away that thought and focused again on opening the safe. He closed his eyes and pictured Tesla in his elegant suit and white gloves working in his lab with brilliant flashes of light surrounding his tall frame.

Next he envisioned an old hotel and a door to one of the rooms. The number on the door was 3327, and then the scene switched back to Tesla in his lab. Jack remembered that the number on the hotel door was Tesla's room number at the hotel New Yorker. That's it! Jack opened his eyes and grabbed the combination dial. *Thirty-three right, twenty seven left..what is the last number?* Jack tried the number thirty-three again and held his breath as he pulled on the handle to open the door. To his amazement, the door unlocked, and Jack pried his fingers behind the door to fully open it. As he began to open the safe door, a trap door underneath him gave way, and Jack found himself tumbling down a slide before landing into a dimly lit tunnel.

Brushing himself off, he saw several light bulbs casting faint light from the tunnel sides. The bulbs were simply stuck into the dirt sides of the tunnel. *What is their power source?* Jack walked up to one of the bulbs and pulled it out from the tunnel wall. The light went out, and he placed it back in the wall to watch it light up again. *What the hell?* He did this several more times with other bulbs, and each lit up the same as the first. Jack smiled as he placed the last bulb back into the wall. *That sonofabitch really did it. Wireless electricity harnessed from the earth. Why did he bury this so deep in the ground? Wouldn't he want the world to have this?*

He put his flashlight back into his pocket to save his battery since he now had dim lighting coming from the bulbs in the wall. Jack's shoes squished in the mud as he walked through the narrow passageway, stopping twice to stretch his stiff back. He followed the tunnel until it made a right bend, and peering around the corner, he saw the path in front of him was pitch black. *Why didn't Tesla light this section?*

Jack pulled out his flashlight and proceeded down the dark corridor, tiptoing slowly step by step. Suddenly, the tunnel was illuminated with a blinding bolt of electricity and a deafening thunderclap in front of him. A bolt of electricity ran across Jack's arm and through his entire body. He was frozen with fear and took a few seconds to look for any serious burns on his body. Seeing none, he pulled out his flashlight to find the source of this power.

Sitting in the middle of the passageway hung a three foot tall Tesla coil suspended in mid-air. Bright bolts of electricity burst forth from the coil every few seconds like it had a life of its own. *Could this be the source of energy for the lights here?* He had read that Tesla demonstrated the safety of taking high voltage currents emitted from his coils. The first jolt he got seemed to pass right through him, and Jack wanted to see for himself if he could touch the coil. The air filled with pops and buzzes of electricity emitting from the coil, and fighting back his instincts, he reached his shaking hand out to it. As soon as his outstretched fingers touched the coil, a huge white flash blinded him as a bolt of electricity threw him against the wall.

Jack opened his eyes and saw a beautiful, bright blue sky above him. He was lying flat on his back on a hard sidewalk with the sounds of traffic whizzing by on a busy street. Rubbing his eyes, he couldn't figure out why it looked like he had been swimming in a mudhole. He sat up and turned around to get an idea of where he was when he realized he was in front of a large church with pedestrians eyeballing him. *Where am I and how the hell did I get here?* When he stood up, a sharp pain stabbed him in the back. A vague memory of falling into a deep hole crept back into his mind, but he was more concerned with where he was at the moment than his sore back.

"Excuse me," said Jack to a lady passing by. "What is the name of this church?"

"The Cathedral of St. John the Divine," she replied eyeing him warily like a homeless person before she quickly moved along.

The huge historic gothic church was a New York landmark that he had passed many times but never entered. He walked up the stairs, opened the front door and immediately felt an eerie, quiet reverence in the empty church, though he was not sure why he had walked in. The massive interior columns stretched upwards towards heaven, and Jack sat in the last row of the pews admiring the architecture. Jack felt the tension in his shoulders melt as he slunk down into the pew and closed his eyes. This was his first time in a church in many years. Jack fell into a deep meditative state when he was startled to hear the loud voice of a stranger calling to him.

"I've been waiting for you, Mr. Cullen," came a voice booming through the church. Jack opened his eyes and looked around the great expanse of the church for the source of this voice. He spotted a thin, gray haired man standing in the vestibule.

"How do you know my name?" a bewildered Jack asked as he stood up, his own voice bouncing off the high church ceiling.

"I've known about you for years, my friend. And I know you are in great danger now. I was sent to protect you. To be your guardian, if you will."

"I'm confused," said Jack as he approached the old man. Jack could see the man was very tall and thin and wore a dark, old fashioned suit. His voice had a faint accent Jack felt was European.

"You still haven't answered my question. How did you know my name?"

"We have a mutual friend."

"And who is that?"

The old man approached Jack and reached out his wrinkled hand for a shake.

"I was sent here by Nikola Tesla himself."

"That's impossible," Jack said with an air of exasperation. "He's been dead since 1943."

"I know that. But Tesla made sure there was a

protector of his secrets from one generation to the next. He passed them down to one trusted friend before he died, and then they have been passed down to me. You are the next chosen one to carry on his legacy."

"This is ridiculous. Why should I believe anything you say?"

The old man stared straight into Jack's eyes. "Because you hold the Tesla papers, and your life is in great danger." A look of panic crossed Jack's face as he tried to remember where they were. "What's the matter? Can't remember where they are, Jack?"

"I...think I remember falling in a hole somewhere, and it was somehow related to Tesla. Next thing I know, I'm lying on the sidewalk out front. Things are a little hazy right now. Who are you, anyway?"

"Arpad Bosnyak is the name. Listen Jack, we have much to talk about, but we are going to have to leave immediately. You are probably being followed."

"I've been followed since the moment I got the Tesla papers, but I doubt anyone knows I'm here now."

"Don't underestimate the diligence of the enemy, Jack. They desperately want the information you have. Some of them want it for themselves, and some of them have much to lose from Tesla's secrets being revealed."

"Who is the enemy?"

"Come with me now and I'll tell you. There is much you need to know. First, I need to help you remember where the Tesla papers are. Let's go out through this side door."

"This church is so beautiful," said Jack as he followed Arpad. "There is something special about this place, but I can't figure out what it is."

"You mean you don't know the significance of this church?"

"No," said Jack.

"This was where Tesla's state funeral was held. I thought you would have known that."

"Now I remember where I was before I came here! I was at Wardenclyffe, and the Tesla papers are in the back of my car. Do you know how to get there?"

"Of course. I have visited there many times. Come, come now," said Arpad as he led Jack to his car. When they pulled out of the parking lot, Jack noticed a woman who looked familiar in a parked car across the street. She pulled out her cell phone and made a call as Arpad's car passed hers, and a chill went up Jack's spine as he had a flashback to his time in the hospital. He recognized the woman in the car as the same nurse who had stitched his ear.

4

Traffic was heavy as Arpad drove through town towards Wardenclyffe to retrieve the Tesla papers from Jack's car. The car seemed to be on automatic pilot as Arpad made his way to Tesla's old laboratory.

"Have you ever been there before?" asked Jack.

"Many times, but not so much anymore. I've been caught by security so many times that they have my picture on file."

"Why do you keep going back?"

"I have tried to find a secret access to the ground underneath the old tower site, but I have not been able to find it."

"That's where I was!" said Jack. "Now I remember! I fell into a sinkhole at the site. I was walking through tunnels and finding light bulbs lit that were not connected to any source. I found a safe and opened it, but I somehow fell through a trap door before seeing the contents. The most amazing thing was the Tesla coil suspended in mid-air. It had sparks emanating from it, and the next thing I know I'm lying on the ground in front of the Cathedral of St. John the Divine."

"Sounds like you were teleported to the church," said Arpad.

"That's impossible. That's a *Star Trek* fantasy."

"Not really. I'm sure you've heard of The Philadelphia Experiment."

"No, I haven't."

"It involved the teleportation of an entire naval ship from Philadelphia to Norfolk, Va. I'd tell you more about it now, but we are getting close to Wardenclyffe. Where is your car?"

Jack craned forward to see around the corner, and he spotted a wrecker ahead getting ready to tow his white Mustang.

"That's it, over there. They're getting ready to tow it. I've got to stop 'em!"

Arpad pulled off the side of the road, and Jack hopped out to approach the driver of the wrecker. The driver was a husky, bearded man with a cigarette dangling from his lips who never looked up at the approaching strangers. He had already hooked up the front of the car with chains to pull it onto his wrecker.

"Excuse me," yelled Jack. "This is my car. You don't have to tow it."

"Sorry sir. I got it all hooked up and ready ta go. I got a call on it that it had been sittin' here all night long. You can come down to this address and pick it up," said the driver as he handed Jack a business card.

"But I'm here now. You don't have to tow this. Here, I'll give you twenty dollars just to unhook it now," said Jack as he pulled out his wallet.

"Nope. I'll make more if I tow it in."

"Mister, you can unhook that car now!" said Arpad as he stood beside his car. The driver stared at the tall, thin old man in a dark suit, and a faint sneer crept on his face.

"You can git back in your car, old man. This car is comin' with me."

Arpad turned and opened his trunk to reach for a two-foot long Tesla coil. He walked towards the driver and gave a reassuring wink to Jack. A few electrical buzzes and zaps could be heard coming from the trunk of Arpad's car.

"How about if I pay you five-hundred dollars right now to unhook this car?" said Arpad.

"Now you're talkin'" said the driver.

"Here, please hold this coil for me while I get my wallet out."

"Sure. What is this thing, anyway? Some kinda mattress coil?" said the driver as Arpad handed it to him.

"No, it's a Tesla coil," said Arpad as he reached into his back pocket. Instead of bringing out his wallet, he pulled out a small rectangular device that looked like a television remote control.

"What's that? That don't look like no wallet...."

Arpad flicked a switch on his remote, and the coil that the driver held electrified causing him to grip it tightly, his teeth clinched. His eyes bugged out while his whole body started to quiver, at first slowly, but then faster.

"What are you doing to him?" yelled Jack.

A loud hum came from the back of Arpad's car along with more zaps and sparking sounds. The driver could not speak or move as if he were being electrocuted. Jack watched as the driver continued to grip the Tesla coil and shake, and a green cloud formed around the driver, enveloping him. When the cloud started to fade away, so did the appearance of the driver. Within a few moments, he had disappeared into thin air. Arpad turned off the remote and placed it back into his pocket.

"What the hell did you just do?" screamed Jack.

"I teleported him, that's all," said Arpad as he made

his way back to his car. He reached in the trunk and turned off a switch causing the loud humming to cease.

"Where did he go?" asked Jack.

"Beats me," shrugged Arpad. "Does it matter?"

"To him it does. My god, where did you get this thing?"

"My Tesla confidant told me about it. You see, I don't need to write anything down. That's how Tesla did it. He had everything right up here," said Arpad pointing to his head.

"Then how come I have some of his papers. He didn't keep everything in his head."

"That's why what you have is so valuable. The only other papers are in the Tesla Museum in Serbia and somewhere on microfilm in government archives. I'm confident the government records of his papers are at Wright-Patterson Air Force Base," said Arpad.

"Right now all I care about is my briefcase. I need to make sure it's still in the car."

Jack unlocked his car and breathed a sigh of relief as he pulled out his briefcase from the trunk. Arpad pulled the chains off the front of Jack's car.

"Follow me back to my house," said Arpad. "Here is my address in case we get separated. You do have GPS don't you?"

"Yes, on my phone."

"Let's get going before I have to teleport someone else."

Jack followed Arpad off the island for another sixty miles west into the countryside. Arpad's car turned onto a long gravel road, and Jack had been watching closely in his rear view mirror to see if he had been followed. It was dusk as they approached a quaint, white two-story country home with a wrap-around porch. A beautiful collie ran out and barked again and again at the sight of both cars. When Arpad got out of his car, the dog jumped up and licked him mercilessly.

"Oh, I missed you too, Buffy," said Arpad as he gave his dog a big hug. Jack grabbed his briefcase and stepped out into the fresh country air. It had been a while since he had breathed in such clean air. The country charm of Arpad's home and the rustling of the wind in the trees reminded him of his boyhood home.

"Quite a spread you have here. How many acres is it?"

"Thirty-three."

"I guess that's no coincidence of being a multiple of three the way Tesla liked, huh?"

"Very good. You have restored my faith in your Tesla knowledge. Please, come in."

Jack walked in and saw a bust of Tesla on a stand in the foyer. The dining room table was covered with papers, books, and research periodicals. A wooden workbench sat in the den with an assortment of gadgets including a three-foot-tall Tesla coil. Above the fireplace in the den was a large painting of the Wardenclyffe tower in its heyday.

"Looks like you have your own research laboratory here on Tesla."

"I guess you could say that," said Arpad. "Can I get you something to drink?"

"Water is fine, thanks." Jack continued to look around as Arpad went to the kitchen. The walls were filled with pictures of Tesla, but missing was any picture related to any family or wife Arpad had.

"Tell me about some of the things you're reading about Tesla these days," said Jack as Arpad handed him a glass of water.

"Please, sit down. I am amazed at the brilliance of Tesla and how advanced his ideas were for his time. It's no wonder he was an outcast."

"You said you were a protector of his legacy, and that job would be handed down to me. What if I don't want that responsibility?"

"Well, you have no choice, really. Possession of that briefcase makes you the natural choice. I have no children, so it has to be you. I have been keeping a record of persons interested in Tesla for years, so when you bought the papers on Craigslist, I knew you were serious."

"So that's how you found me. I've read the Tesla papers in this briefcase, and they give a convincing argument for the distribution of free electricity to the world. I don't have the actual device to generate it, but I feel confident I could build one with some help. Could you help me build it?"

"No need to. I already have one."

"You have a free electricity generator?" asked Jack.

"Of course."

"Did you make it yourself or did you get ideas from those sold on the internet."

"Oh, those on the internet are all garbage. They claim to make free electricity and use Tesla's name to promote themselves, but none of them work. Trust me, I've tried them all. Would you like to see it?"

"Yes, of course I would!" Jack couldn't believe he was going to see the world's first free electricity generating device. He had seen the mysteriously lit bulbs underground at Wardenclyffe, but he wasn't sure if the Tesla coil was the power source.

"Come with me," said Arpad as he grabbed the Tesla coil from the table.

Jack followed Arpad out to his back porch. It was now dark outside, and the only light came from the moon and stars. Arpad walked down the steps and stuck one end of the Tesla coil into the ground as Buffy looked on. At that exact moment, his entire back yard lit up with hundreds of light bulbs. Rows and rows of light bulbs were scattered throughout the yard with enough light to play a game of baseball.

"What is the power source of these bulbs?" asked Jack.

"Radiant energy from the earth. It's all around us."

Jack bent down to pick up a light bulb from the ground, and the bulb continued to burn brightly, much to his wonder and amazement. There were no wires attached to it just as he had discovered at Wardenclyffe.

"This is just what I saw at Wardenclyffe underground. This is fantastic! Why have you not told anyone about this? This would change the world!"

"Because the world was not ready for this. Besides, I'm too old to go through the mayhem this would cause. Do you know how many people will want to suppress free electricity?"

"The Middle East, for starters. Their whole way of life is based on oil money."

"Exactly. And what is the nationality of those men who are trying to kill you."

"I never told you anyone was trying to kill me," said Jack. "How did you know that?"

"It only makes sense. They've been looking to collect and squash Tesla's ideas for decades. Our government knows all about it, but they aren't letting this information out. Saudi Arabia would pay dearly for the papers you hold."

"This is too important to be kept a secret any longer. We've got to get this information out," said Jack.

"I used to be as gung-ho as you are," said Arpad scratching his chin. "Get ready to be attacked on all fronts. No one will believe you. Believe me, I've tried. I approached the U.S. Department of Energy years ago with this. I gave them everything, specs, a working model. They did squat with it. Hell, they've had Tesla's papers on teleportation since his death. The government doesn't want this information in the wrong hands. Can you imagine a terrorist organization with a teleporter?"

"I understand. But what is the problem with free energy? Everybody benefits from that," said Jack.

"Sure they would. But energy companies lose. Coal mining would stop and all fossil fuels that make electricity would be shut down. Then there are all the suppliers of these businesses that would disappear. In the Middle East their whole way of life is predicated on oil revenue. The U.S. government does not want to destabilize that region any more than it is now. So free energy gets stuffed under the mattress forever. But there's one other thing the U.S. government doesn't want to ever be revealed that they learned from Tesla".

"What is that?" asked Jack.

"Tesla was convinced he was contacted by

intelligent beings from outer space while he was conducting experiments in Colorado Springs in 1899. He kept getting transmissions that he couldn't explain away to anything else. He died with indisputable proof that we are not alone in the universe. And the government has kept this evidence under tight security at Wright-Patterson Air Force base in Ohio ever since. No way are they going to let this information out. The only way it ever would get out is from the inside."

"So, do you know someone there?"

"I used to work there."

"So you've got contacts there still?"

"Only one and I haven't talked to her in years. I'm not sure she's still there anymore."

"You should call her."

"And ask her to do what? Steal documents from the U.S. Government? She could be tried for treason. And why would we want this information anyway? The world is full of crackpots who have claimed to see aliens."

"We could use it as leverage. We agree to not release the information about extra-terrestrial contact in exchange for releasing Tesla's free energy device to the world. That should be our ultimate goal."

"Yes, that is what Tesla would have wanted. The poor guy never knew how to keep money. Hell, he tore up several of his patents so his partner Westinghouse wouldn't have to pay him. That way Westinghouse could keep his business afloat. Tesla lost millions doing that. You could earn a fortune selling the free energy device."

"I know I could," said Jack. "But I'm not in this for the money. I promised a police officer I'd go in with him on the sale of this. But I needed his protection, so I agreed to split money with him. This information will not be sold at any cost."

Arpad smiled. "Good. You are just the man Tesla would have wanted. Poor cop thinks he's a millionaire already."

"He did save my life. He's a good man," said Jack.

"Listen, we are all in danger for the information we possess. But I don't see how we could possibly get away with stealing Tesla's secret papers from a secure government air force base," said Arpad.

"I've seen from you, first hand, what teleportation can do. Let's call your old contact there."

Arpad fidgeted and stared at the floor.

"What's the matter, you're acting like you don't wanna call an old friend."

"She broke my heart once. I don't think I could bear to see her again," Arpad said with a pained look on his face.

"I'm sorry," said Jack. "It's never too late, you know."

"Yes it is. I'm way too old now."

"Don't give up on love just because you're old. The world needs this, Arpad. You owe it to humanity to give it to them. That's what Tesla would have wanted."

"Tesla tried. But everybody thought he was a crazy old man who talked to outer space voices. There are many things that Tesla worked on that nobody knows about. He spoke of sending pictures and news wirelessly over the air in the early 1900's. And I've heard that the government has a working prototype of a flying saucer conceived from the papers they confiscated after he died."

"What? Who told you that? Have you ever seen it?"

"No. But my old friend there whispered about it to me. She ran across some classified papers on it but never told anyone what she saw. She would have been fired since she didn't have the proper security clearance."

"That's incredible," said Jack.

"He didn't call it a flying saucer. He called it an anti-gravity device. No one believed any of them would work."

"You mean the government could be responsible for all the UFO sightings over the years? No wonder they don't want to talk about it. They didn't acknowledge that Area 51 existed for years. What is the name of your lady friend there? I'm gonna call her myself."

"Magda. But don't call her. I'll do it myself."

"You will?"

"I just need to find out if she is still even alive. I gave up on love a long time ago and have gotten used to being alone. Like me, Tesla was a loner and never married. He was closest to a special pigeon in his apartment in New York and was devastated when it died. He would spend hours sitting on a park bench feeding pigeons. They flocked to him whenever he came to visit them, and he was closer to those birds than he ever was to a human. Tesla was awarded the Thomas Edison award for contributions to science, and he had to be begged to accept the award. On the night of the award presentation, Tesla was nowhere to be found. A friend knew where to look and found him in Bryant Park feeding hundreds of pigeons. Tesla only returned to accept the award after his friend convinced him that he had to go back."

"You know that Tesla and Edison didn't get along," said Jack.

"That's putting it mildly. There was a huge battle at the turn of the century over AC vs DC. Edison was a proponent of DC because he deemed it much safer than the higher voltage AC current. Edison even electrocuted elephants in public with high voltage AC current to frighten people about its dangers. Edison was a tireless inventor, but he was proven dead wrong about AC electricity. Tesla won the battle after his partnership with Westinghouse produced hydroelectric energy from Niagara Falls."

"History will work out for Tesla's ideas in the long run, but in the short run, we've got to get more of the Tesla papers. And the sooner the better with those guys on my heels. I think you need to call Magda right away."

Arpad scratched Buffy's head and stared off into the unwired field of lights before him. "I will, Jack. But not right now. We'll look at your papers in the morning, but I'm too tired tonight. Let's just enjoy the lights."

Both men stood still and admired their own magic light show. Jack noticed the frogs from the nearby pond stopped croaking as soon as the lights lit up as if they, too, were in a trance.

5

Jack was awakened by the sound of Buffy barking in the hallway outside his bedroom. Opening the door, he smelled smoke and ran to Arpad's bedroom.

"Arpad, I think there's a fire! Get up!"

Arpad jumped out of bed and joined Jack in a race down the hall. They saw flames coming from the den in the back of the house as Buffy barked and ran in circles.

"Call 911!" yelled Jack. Arpad reached for the phone but got no dial tone.

"It's dead. Where is your cell?" asked Arpad.

"It's in my room," yelled Jack as he rushed to his bedroom while Arpad grabbed his fire extinguisher from the kitchen and sprayed the flames as they spread to the curtains. The flames grew too big for the small kitchen extinguisher, and Arpad's hair caught on fire as he got too close to the ever higher flames. Smoke had now spread through the entire house.

"I've got 911 on the line. What's your street address?" asked Jack as Arpad ran to the kitchen to put his hair out.

"24 County Road 624," replied Arpad as he placed a wet towel on his head. Jack repeated the address to the dispatcher.

"We can't stay in here any longer. Get your Tesla papers and let's get outta here."

"What about all your Tesla artifacts?"

"They're protected. Don't worry. Grab your papers and let's go."

Jack ran down the hallway and strained to see the entry to his bedroom through the thick smoke. He grabbed his papers, wallet and a pair of jeans and ran back to the den, unable to spot Arpad anywhere.

"Arpad! Where are you?"

"Down here on the floor. I couldn't take the smoke anymore."

Jack got down on all fours and crawled towards the front door. Reaching up, he touched the doorknob and was relieved that it was cool. He stood up, opened the door, and helped Arpad up off the floor. With Jack's arm around Arpad's shoulder, they stumbled out the front door, each of them coughing from the smoke.

"My car is on the side of the house over here. Follow me," said Jack as he slipped on his jeans and grabbed his keys from his pocket. Arpad ran in his pajamas and grabbed his muddy work boots which were sitting on the front stoop. Jack felt like the heat from the flames was going to melt his skin as he tossed his briefcase in the back seat and hopped in the car. He sped to the end of the driveway to await the fire truck.

"You okay?"

Arpad pulled the wet towel off his head and looked into the mirror. The smell of burnt hair filled the car.

"Good thing I didn't have much hair left," said Arpad as he saw what remained of his singed hair.

"You're joking and you just got your hair burned off your head. And why in the hell did your house just catch on fire?"

"I don't think it was an accident. I think your Middle Eastern friends followed us here," said Arpad.

"What? I don't remember seeing anyone follow us?"

"Remember, you hold information they want to destroy. I bet they're sitting in a car close by waiting to see if we survived. Let's lay low for a while."

Jack heard the distant sound of sirens coming towards them. Flames were now shooting through the roof.

"I think your house is gonna be a total loss. Are you sure your Tesla artifacts are safe?"

"Yes, I always keep them in a fireproof safe in the basement. I never knew my house would burn up, but I thought it a good idea to have a safe nonetheless. I can't believe it's gone."

Two fire trucks and an ambulance turned into the driveway, and Jack waved them on. By the time the firemen got out, the roof had collapsed as Arpad looked helplessly back at the house he had lived in for the past thirty years. A tear rolled down his face as he turned his head away. Loud pops emanated from the flames while firefighters struggled to contain the fire. An hour later the firefighters were putting the last of the flames out. Only one side of the house remained standing as the rest was a smoldering pile of charcoal.

"Sir, we're going to saturate this fire until it is completely out. Under no circumstances are you to go in to retrieve anything. It's way too dangerous. There's not much left anyway. And we detected a strong gasoline smell along the back of your house. Did you store any gas at the back of your home?"

"No, I didn't."

"Do you need any medical assistance?"

"No, I'm fine. Just a little hair got burned."

"Well, this fire needs to be investigated. There are definite signs of an accelerant being used to start this fire. I think you should call the police."

"Oh, my. I don't know why there would be a gas smell. I'll definitely contact the authorities."

"Do you have a place to stay tonight? A neighbor perhaps?" asked the fireman.

"Yes, I do. Thank you very much for all your help."

"Just doing our job, sir. I'm glad there was no one in the home besides the two of you. You're very lucky to be alive. We'll be finished shortly."

Jack took Arpad by the arm and walked down the driveway.

"You were right. Those guys did this. How are we gonna make it back into your basement to get your belongings from your safe?"

"We'll go in right after the firefighters leave. Where's Buffy?"

"I don't know. She must have gotten scared and run away."

"We can't leave here until we've unlocked my safe and found Buffy. Those men will be back here to search, I promise you. We can walk down the stairs to the basement. From what I've seen, there's not much damage down there except tons of water."

The firefighters finished their spray of water on Arpad's home and wrapped yellow caution tape around it. Arpad and Jack waved at the firefighters as they climbed in their fire trucks and drove down the long, winding driveway. After they were safely out of sight, Arpad pulled the tape up and crawled under.

"Are you coming?"

"I guess I am. This can't be more dangerous than holding the Tesla papers."

Jack followed Arpad under the yellow tape and tiptoed among the still hot ruins. Each step was accompanied by a loud crunch of burnt material under their feet. The smoky smell stung Jack's nostrils.

"Here's the stairwell down to the basement. It's covered with debris and water, but I think we can make it down okay. Don't touch anything because it's still hot. Good thing I found my work boots."

Arpad pushed debris down the stairs of the small basement now filled with several inches of water. Jack made his way down and saw an old blue sofa soaked with water and covered with charred wood.

"The safe is behind that sofa. Help me pull it out."

Jack grabbed the waterlogged sofa to expose a hidden door. Arpad slid the door back to reveal a four-foot tall safe, and he bent down to see the combination lock.

"Shine your phone on the lock so I can see", said Arpad as he turned the dial left, right and back again. The door opened, and Arpad pulled out two three-foot tall Tesla coils, a nondescript small square metal box, some papers rolled up in a tube, and what looked like a writing pen but longer.

"Thank God for this safe! I would have lost everything," said Arpad.

"What is all this? I recognize the coil, but what's the small box?" asked Jack.

Arpad and Jack froze when they heard a car door shut outside. Jack placed his finger over his mouth while motioning to Arpad to stand still. Jack climbed up the stairs and peered out from debris around the top of the stairwell when he saw two Middle Eastern men in suits approaching the house. He ducked down and made his way back to Arpad in the basement.

"It's them," whispered Jack.

"Okay. I'm ready. Go hide in the back. I'll be behind this sofa."

Jack dragged his feet through the water to keep quiet while Arpad put everything back in the safe except for the pen-like device. Crouching behind a soggy stuffed chair, Jack heard voices in Arabic mixed with the crunching of feet on burned remnants above them. A voice got closer until one man stood at the top of the stairwell. Jack steadied his breathing and felt his heartbeat quicken. They didn't have time to plan, and what could an old man kneeling behind a sofa in his pajamas really do? One footstep landed on the stairwell, and then two. Jack could see the legs of a man, and step by step more of his body appeared as he crept down the steps. Jack could see he had a gun drawn when a piece of debris fell off the stairs and splashed in front of the sofa. The man pointed his gun in the direction of the splash but did not fire. Arpad was no more than twenty feet from the bottom of the stairs, but kneeling down, he could not see what was happening. He heard the splash of a footstep and felt the wave move against his feet under the sofa. As the intruder took another step towards him, Arpad raised his pen and activated a laser beam at the man's head. The man screamed, dropped his gun and grabbed at his now burning face. Jack's eyes widened as he saw the red laser beam burn their attacker.

The man turned to run up the stairs, and Arpad kept the beam on him as he continued screaming and holding his face. The second man heard the screams and came to the top of the stairs only to see his partner in agony with flesh melting off his face like butter. His screams were sickening, unlike any Jack had heard before. The burning faced man only made it halfway up the stairs before he collapsed with a splash on the concrete floor. The second man wanted no part of whatever destroyed his partner's face and ran back to his car. Arpad and Jack heard tires spinning and a car speeding away. Jack couldn't look at the deformed face of the motionless man on the floor.

"What the hell did you do to him?" asked Jack.

"You have witnessed the successful operation of the world's smallest particle beam accelerator. Back in Tesla's day it was called the "Death Ray.""

"Did you make it yourself?"

"I had some help from my friend at Wright-Patterson. She sent me a drawing from some of the Tesla archives, and I had some help from another friend in building it. I'd never used it on a person, though."

"Good thing. How do you get so much power from such a small device?"

"It's too complicated to explain now. Here, take this Tesla coil for me," said Arpad as he reached into the safe.

"How are you going to explain a dead body with a burned up face in the basement of your home that was just destroyed by a couple Middle Eastern terrorists?"

"I don't know," shrugged Arpad.

"Well, you've got an answer for everything else. Oh, and the firefighters said we should call the police. They're going to come eventually. What do we do with this body?"

"I've never dealt with a dead body, and I'm not about to start now. We've got more important things to think about. Let's get out of here."

Arpad and Jacked grabbed everything from the safe and stepped over the dead man on the floor and climbed the steps outside. Arpad retrieved his car from the end of the driveway, opened his trunk and put in the briefcase and Tesla inventions.

"Where is Buffy? I can't leave without her. Buffy! Bufffyyy! Come here girl. She never liked sirens and the fire truck scared her to death. Buffy!"

"There she is," yelled Jack as Buffy raced from the thick woods. Arpad got down on his knees and hugged Buffy as she jumped into his arms and licked his face.

"Oh, you scared me girl. Hop in the car and let's go."

"Where exactly are we going?" asked Jack

"Wright-Patterson Air Force Base. Where else?"

6

Magda Chabornik had sat at the same desk at Wright-Patterson Air Force Base for the last thirty-eight years, and she now stared past her computer screen to the pond outside her window. She had just notified her boss of her retirement at the end of the month. Her mind drifted from her two children who had moved away, to her late husband's death, to the many instances of her being passed over for promotions by yet another man. The phone ringing on her desk startled her from her daydream.

"Wright-Patterson. This is Magda. May I help you?"

The caller did not answer.

"Hello, this is Magda. May I help you?"

"Magda...this is Arpad."

Magda covered her mouth and leaned back in her chair. Her heartbeat doubled its pace.

"Arpad Bosnyak? Is that really you?"

"Yes, it is."

"I...I don't know what to say. How many years has it been?"

"Too many to count. Thirty-something? How are you?"

"I am fine. My kids are both married and have moved away. I've got a grandson due in two months. My husband died two years ago from cancer, and I just announced my retirement at the end of this month."

"Wow! Much has happened. I'm sorry about your husband."

"Thank you. He was a wonderful man. What about you?"

"I never married. I met a woman once who I thought I could spend my life with, but I got my heart broken."

"I'm sorry. You know, it's so good to hear your voice again. I always loved your voice."

"Magda... the woman who broke my heart was you."

"I...I've always wanted to apologize to you, but I didn't know how to do it. Then you left here, and I didn't know how to find you. I even looked for you on Facebook after my husband died, but you weren't there. I guess it may be too late for an apology, but I'll do it anyway. Arpad, I'm so sorry for the way it ended between us. It was just not right, and you deserved so much better. I've thought about you often over the years and wondered what had happened to you."

"Well, I've thought of you a lot, too. But I had to move on with my career. I got a job with the CIA and did a lot of work in electrical systems for spy satellites. I can't believe I'm talking to you now. It seems like we've never been apart."

"Yes, it does. I know this may be very presumptuous on my part, but I would love to see you again."

"It's funny you should say that because I could use your help. But I need to talk to you about this privately. Can I call you at home tonight?"

"Yes, my number is 937-642-2839."

"Okay, I'll call you around 7p.m. Is that okay?"

"Yes, yes, that's fine. I look forward to it."

"Me too. Goodbye."

"Goodbye."

Arpad handed Jack's phone back to him as they drove on the interstate towards Dayton.

"She still loves me. I can tell."

"You just want to get back with her, don't you? This Tesla stuff is just a ploy," Jack said, smiling.

"I can assure you it is not a ploy. My purpose is to obtain documents that have been kept secret too long. If I rekindle an old flame, then that is just a bonus."

"Before you go see her, we first have to get you some clothes. You can't go in your pajamas."

"Yes, you are right. Stop at the first Wal-Mart you see. I'm not picky."

"You sure you wanna go in a Wal-Mart dressed like that?"

"Are you kidding? You ever been in a Wal-Mart? No one will notice," said Arpad.

Jack drove for five hours and stopped in a small town in western Pennsylvania to spend the night. He checked in at a motel where they allowed pets and gave Arpad his car to take to Wal-Mart for clothes. As he waved goodbye, Jack noticed a familiar car in the farthest corner of the parking lot. He decided to get a closer look at the person in the car while walking Buffy. He approached the car and memorized the New York license plate. A young, blonde woman was on her cell phone, and he recognized her as the nurse who treated him in the hospital after he was shot in the ear. He let Buffy pee in the grass nearby, then walked to her car and stood outside her window. Her eyes widened like saucers when she looked up, and she hung the phone up and cracked her window open slightly.

"May I help you?"

"Yes. You can stop following me."

"What do you mean?"

"You're the same nurse who stitched my ear up in

New York a few weeks ago. It's no coincidence you are here in this parking lot, so don't give me any bullshit answers. Just tell me why you are following me. I've got your license plate number, and if you leave I'll report you to the police for stalking. So, why are you following me?"

"I'm not following you. I do recognize you as a patient, though. Did you get shot in the ear?"

"Yes, you know very well that was me. I saw you following me another time outside Cathedral St. John the Divine in New York. Now I see you again here in the parking lot of a motel in Pennsylvania. Don't insult my intelligence. Who sent you here?"

"No one. I have some relatives in the area. That's why I'm here."

"Uh huh. Are you sure it has nothing to do with the fact that I have some papers your people want?"

"And what papers would that be?"

"The Tesla papers."

"Who is Tesla?"

"Nikola Tesla. He was a famous scientist who died in 1943, but I think you know exactly who he is. Who sent you to follow me?"

"I don't know what the hell you're talking about. I've never even heard of this Tesla guy. I've had enough of this. I'm going now."

As the woman started her car, Jack took Buffy by the leash and stood in front of her car.

"You're going to have to run over Buffy and me to get out of here. A nurse would never intentionally hurt anyone, would they? How about this dog? Do you wanna be known as a dog killer?"

"Get out of the way or I'll run you over," she screamed.

"No you won't," said Jack as he spotted Arpad pull into the parking lot and motioned for him to come over.

The woman put the car in reverse and tried to speed backwards away from Jack and Buffy. The tires spun and the car backed down an embankment into a muddy ditch. She spun her tires and spewed mud, but the car would not budge.

"What happened here? Why did she back straight into that ditch?" asked Arpad as he got out of his car dressed in new clothes.

"She has been following me and I confronted her. She denied it and tried to get away."

"So you were going to let her run over Buffy?"

"No, she would never do that. People will run over another human before they'll harm a dog."

"Good girl, Buffy," said Arpad as he knelt down to hug her.

"Pull out your laser. We've got to convince this lady to talk to us."

"Are you sure we need that?" asked Arpad.

"We need some leverage. She won't talk. I don't intend to use it on her, but we need to show her what it can do."

"Okay. But I don't want to hurt a lady," said Arpad as he pulled the pen out of his coat pocket.

"Nice threads. Magda will love it."

"I sure didn't buy them for you."

"Oh, be quiet. Let's go help this woman get out of her car and talk to her."

The nurse opened her door and tried to run when she saw them approach her. She slipped in the mud, and Jack grabbed her legs.

"Now, why don't you get up and we'll help you clean up. Give me your cell phone, and we can talk back in our room."

"You think I'm gonna go into a motel room with two complete strangers? No way."

"I think you will. Arpad, show her what's in your pocket." Arpad pulled out his pen and held it up for her to see.

"Oh, I'm so scared of a pen. What are you gonna do, write on me?"

Without saying a word, Arpad aimed the pen at a beer bottle lying in the bottom of the ditch and activated the laser. The bottle shattered into bits and broken glass sprayed back in their direction. Jack pulled fragments of glass out of his arm and checked on Arpad.

"I think I'm okay, but I don't think she is," said Arpad pointing to the woman who had multiple cuts from shards of glass.

"You have to let us help you now. You are badly injured. I had no idea the glass would spray back on us," said Arpad.

"What is your name?" asked Jack.

"Ann Lastrapes."

"Please, let us help you. We did not intend to hurt you. Let us help you up."

Arpad and Jack took each took an arm and pulled Ann off the ground. She screamed in agony when she put weight on her left leg. Jack grimaced when he saw a one-inch shard of glass sticking out of her thigh.

"We may need to get you to a hospital," said Jack.

"I'll be the judge of that. I'm the nurse here."

They both carried her across the parking lot to their room and laid her down on the bed. Buffy licked her in the face, and she smiled and petted her on the head.

"Give me a washcloth, please," said Ann.

Arpad grabbed a cloth from the bathroom and handed it to her.

"I don't think it's in too deep," she said, and without a warning, she yanked the glass out, causing Jack and Arpad to wince.

"You'll need to take my jeans off to look at the wound. Can you help me take them off?"

Arpad and Jack looked at each other to see who would go first.

"It's okay, I'm a nurse you jackasses. I've seen things you've never seen before. Just take it slow, and bring me a warm washcloth and towel."

Jack helped her take her jeans off while Arpad soaked a washcloth in hot water. Blood streaked down her leg from a one-inch gouge in her thigh. Arpad compressed the wound and placed a towel over her legs while Jack pulled a few small pieces of glass from her neck.

"Just hold still," said Jack as he gingerly pulled out more glass.

"You're a brave woman," said Arpad.

"Not really. You guys are the brave ones. You've got some important papers."

"And how do you know that, Ann," asked Arpad.

"I was hired to follow you."

"Who hired you," asked Jack.

"I'd rather not say as my life might be in danger, but let's say that they have a vested interest in the information you have."

"Do you know where we are headed now?" asked Arpad.

"No, I don't."

"Good. We are on an important mission and can't have anyone tail us. So, what are we supposed to do with you?" asked Jack.

"Take me with you," said Ann.

"Why would we do that? You have given us no reason to trust you. You could call your employer and give us up. Tell us who hired you, and then some trust can begin," said Jack.

Ann sat up on the bed and cleaned some more blood off her leg.

"I don't know who exactly I work for, but it has to do with an oil conglomerate out of Saudi Arabia. They told me that you were going to use this information against them, and it was in the interest of Saudi Arabia and the U.S. to keep this information from leaking. They told me as little as possible."

"Why did they hire you? Do you work for the CIA?"

"I used to but I was outed. It made a big stink a few years ago, so I had to resign."

"I read about that in the paper. That was you?" asked Jack.

"Yes, and it was awful. My area of expertise was Saudi Arabia. I had a number of high level contacts there, so they called me to follow you guys. I really don't know what you guys are up to, but they offered me $25,000 to tail you, and I'm divorced and need the money."

"Do you know that there have been three attempts on my life in the last few weeks?" asked Jack.

"No, I'm sorry. They didn't tell me anything about killing you. All they wanted to know was where you were."

"And then they relayed that information over to some nice little hit men who tried to kill both of us. Arpad's house is burned down, and I've been attacked twice. Fortunately, two of the three guys that were sent after me are dead. But, they'll be back, probably with others."

"I swear I had no idea they were trying to kill you."

"That's okay. You were just doing your job. Now we have a job to do, too. I have to go call my friend at Wright-Patterson now," said Arpad.

"You're going to Wright-Patterson? I spent six months there on an assignment," said Ann.

Jack and Arpad looked at each other and knew they were each thinking the same thing.

"Arpad, go make your call to your lady friend, and I'll bring Ann up to speed on what we're doing."

"Okay, I'll be calling from the car," said Arpad.

Jack proceeded to spend the next half hour telling Ann all about Tesla's discovery of free energy and the government cover up of UFOs. He told her that they were going to break into Wright-Patterson with the help of Arpad's connection on the inside there.

"You think you can break into Wright-Patterson?" Ann laughed. "You're crazy. That base has 5,000 people protecting it and is home to the 88th air base wing. It's a major military installation, and you think you and an old man can break in there with the help of one probably very old woman on the inside?"

"Yes, but only because we have something they don't have."

"And what might that be?"

"Working prototypes of actual Tesla technology. That little device that blasted the bottle and injured you is one of them."

"How did you get hold of that? Anything related to Tesla is highly classified."

"Arpad had them handed down to him from a man who knew Tesla. Tesla entrusted his technology to only one person who is supposed to keep passing it to the next generation until the world is ready for it. I bought my information off of Craigslist."

"You've got to be kidding. How in the hell can you buy top secret information from Nikola Tesla off of Craigslist."

"The seller didn't know what she had. Her father worked in the same hotel that Tesla lived in, and he got hold of some papers that Tesla sold to pay off his bills. Pretty incredible, huh?"

"I'd never believe it unless I saw them myself," said Ann.

"Well, take a look for yourself," said Jack as he pulled the yellowing papers out of his briefcase and spread them out for her on the bed. Ann scanned the first page and turned several more pages inspecting the diagrams for the use of free energy.

"This is unbelievable. I got to see a little of the Tesla stuff they were working on at Wright-Patterson, but none of it had to do with free energy. Most of it what I saw had to do with laser guided weaponry."

"There's a lot the government has done with Tesla's work that we don't know about. But I guess we'll find out once we get there. We sure could use your help."

Ann removed the washcloth from her leg wound and saw the bleeding had begun to slow. "I'm going to need some bandages. Can you go to my car and get the first aid kit out of my trunk? Us nurses are always prepared. I think the keys are still in the car."

"I don't mind at all," said Jack as he grabbed his jacket and headed to the parking lot. Ann turned to the Tesla papers on the bed and continued reading. Her eyes scanned to a quote at the bottom of the last few pages. The quote was from an Oct. 15, 1911 interview Tesla gave to the *New York Herald Tribune*.

"The flying machine of the future —my flying machine— will be heavier than air, but it will not be an aero-plane. It will have no wings. It will be substantial, solid, stable. You might see it on the ground and you would never guess that it was a flying machine. Yet it will be able to move at will through the air in any direction with perfect safety, at higher speeds than have yet been reached, regardless of weather and oblivious of 'holes in the air' or downward currents...It can remain absolutely stationary in the air, even in wind, for a great length of time. Its lifting power will not depend upon any such delicate devices as the bird has to employ, but upon positive mechanical action. The application of this principle will give the world a flying machine unlike anything that has ever been suggested before. It will have no planes, no screw propellers or devices of any kind hitherto used. It will be small and compact, excessively swift, and, above all, perfectly safe in the greatest storm. It can be built of any size and can carry any weight that may be desired."

Ann felt the hair on her arm stand on end as she read. She was startled when both Arpad and Jack opened the door to the room.

"I'm in. I want to be a part of this. I had heard rumors of flying disc technology, but now it all makes sense."

"You know the Nazis used Tesla's ideas on anti-gravity to work on a prototype of a flying disc. They were years ahead of everyone in research, and they were very close to coming up with a working model. Tesla was only interested in his inventions being used for the betterment of man or defensive purposes. Thank God we defeated them when we did," said Arpad.

"Now we've got two women working with us," said Arpad as he high-fived Jack. "But how can we be sure to trust you. You've been spying on us for weeks."

"Listen, I don't need the money that bad. I'm more interested in bringing Tesla's ideas to the world. That's a greater legacy than anything I can think of."

"Okay, I'll trust you until you give me a reason not to," said Arpad with his arms crossed in front of his body.

"That's not exactly a reassuring vote of confidence in me. So your lady friend agreed, huh. I don't know how we're going to do this. We'll all probably be shot dead. Someone has to stay back in case something goes wrong. Is that enough proof to you that I'm serious, Arpad? I think Jack should stay," said Ann.

"Whoa, we don't have to decide that now," said Jack.

"Maybe she's right," said Arpad. "You're the chosen one to carry on for Tesla."

"You guys are acting like we're all gonna die," said Jack. "That is not going to happen."

"We're all going to die someday, so we might as well choose under what circumstances," said Arpad. "I've lived a good long life, and I can die easy knowing Jack is there to carry the torch for Tesla."

Outside in the far corner of the parking lot, a car with a lone man inside turned its lights off.

7

Officer Wayne Claiborne finished reading the paper in the darkness early on Saturday morning. He rubbed his eyes, yawned and quietly put his dishes away to not disturb his sleeping wife and kids. Sleep had eluded him most nights since the disappearance of his new friend Jack. Wayne logged back onto his work laptop and continued his hunt in police reports about missing persons.

"Still looking for Jack, huh?" said Betty as she stood behind her husband in the dark.

"You scared the crap outta me!"

"Well, you keep waking me every time you roll out of bed. Why can't you stay asleep anymore? Are you too busy thinking about that man that almost got us killed?"

"I can't stop thinkin' about him. There's no trace of Jack anywhere in police reports. I've researched this guy Tesla to see if I can come up with any hints of where to find Jack, but I'm at a dead end."

"Sounds to me like you're chasing another pipe dream. Remember that network marketing scheme you got into before? You were gonna make us rich from that, too, and look how that worked out. We're still paying off bills from buying magnets for your health. When are you gonna learn?"

"This doesn't require any investment of money, just my time."

"Uh, huh. Why don't you stop wasting your time? You're never gonna find that man. I think he's bad news, honey. If you ask me, you should just forget about him."

"I didn't ask you."

"So now you're getting smart with me? I oughta..."

"Daddy! Wanna come play the XBox with me?" asked Derrick as he stood in the doorway in his pajamas rubbing his eyes.

"Of course I do," said Wayne as he jumped from the chair, grabbed his son, and twirled him in the air.

"You're just trying to avoid an argument," said Betty putting her hands on her hips.

Wayne ignored her and sat on the floor in front of the television with his son.

"I heard you and Mommy talking about Mr. Jack. I liked him. Where is he now?"

"I really don't know, son. I've been looking for him."

"I liked that car ride Mommy did when he was with us. That was fun!"

"Oh, yeah. That was quite a ride."

"I liked reading about that Tesla guy he was talking about. Do you know much about him?"

"Yes, but only since I met Jack," said Wayne as he played on the Xbox.

"Killed you again, Daddy," screamed Derrick raising his arms.

"Yes you did. Two out of three?"

"Yup. Let's go."

"Got you again!" screamed Derrick after he won the next game.

"I think I've had enough. You're too good for me," said Wayne as he sat down to read the paper while Derrick continued. He usually started with the sports section, but an article caught his eye on the front page. The headline read *Man Found Dead in Mysterious House Fire*. Wayne leaned over the paper to read about the total loss of a house belonging to Arpad Bosnyak. A dead Middle-Eastern man was found in the basement with unusual injuries. The forty-year old home on 33 acres was located 60 miles west of New York, and the owner was nowhere to be found. A firefighter stated that he spoke to Mr. Bosnyak the morning of the fire and told him that arson was suspected. Another man was seen with Mr. Bosnyak at the scene, and the identity of the victim was unconfirmed. The dead man found in the basement had injuries inconsistent with anything that he had seen before. The firefighter stated the deceased had a "face melted like butter, but the rest of his body was unburned. It was crazy."

Wayne hopped out of his chair, pulled on some jeans and a shirt and headed to his car.

"Just going into the office to do some paperwork, honey."

"What? Are you crazy? Why are you going in on a Saturday? You haven't done that in years. And what kind of paperwork is so important that you have to leave your family?"

"Something has come up that I need to attend to. I can't tell you what right now," said Wayne.

"You better not be looking for Jack or you're in big trouble. That man caused us way too much trouble..." Wayne could not make out Betty's last words as he closed the door of his cruiser. He drove straight to the police station and looked up the address of the suspicious fire he saw in the paper. Logging on his computer, he found the address of Arpad Bosnyak and did a criminal history search on him. Finding nothing, he hopped in his car and headed to the scene of the fire. Wayne wasn't sure what he would say to Jack if he saw him, but he also wasn't sure if he was going on a wild goose chase. After a two hour drive, Wayne's GPS directed him to a long dirt driveway. Driving under the tree canopy to Arpad's home, Wayne saw a car in the driveway and a man walking in front of the remnants of a burned home. Wayne parked his police cruiser and approached a short balding man in jeans.

"Hello, may I help you officer?"

"Yes sir. I'm looking for the owner to ask him a few questions. Do you know of his whereabouts?"

"No sir. I'm an arson specialist with the fire department. I was asked to determine what the cause of the fire was."

"And have you come to a conclusion?"

"Possibly. I did detect remnants of an accelerant at the back of the house."

"Mind if I look around a little bit?"

"Oh, help yourself. Just be careful. I wouldn't try going down those basement steps. They almost collapsed after they removed the body. They said that guys' face was burned off. Pretty sick."

"Yes, it is." Wayne climbed over some debris at the front of the house and stepped past what was once the front door. Most of the furniture was burned beyond recognition, and he tripped on something on the floor, falling down hard on his side. Wayne opened his eyes and found himself staring into the face of a blackened statue. He saw letters engraved at the bottom of the bust and rubbed them clean to reveal the letters TESLA.

Wayne scrambled to his feet and bent down to pick up the bust. Staring into the eyes of the great inventor, Wayne knew he was on the right track to find Jack. Who else would carry a bust of Nikola Tesla in their home unless there was a strong connection to the inventor? Wayne put the bust down, stood up and brushed himself off as he spotted the arson investigator writing his report.

"Excuse me, have you seen or talked to the owner yet?" asked Wayne.

"No sir. No one has to my knowledge. I'm not even sure his insurance company knows. Kinda weird if you ask me."

"Yes, it is. Have you heard anything about the identity of the dead man?"

"You're the police, you should know."

"I'm not active on this case. I live in New York."

"What the hell are you doin' here then? Not just any cop can come here askin' questions."

"I don't have to explain myself to you. I've seen all I've needed to see anyway," said Wayne as he walked back to his car. The short balding man followed his car while scribbling down his license plate on a notepad.

Wayne wracked his brain thinking of where Jack could be, and he started back home trying to think of something to tell his wife. She was not going to be happy, but it would be okay with her if he came away with his share of profits from Tesla's free energy device. Wayne's mind raced as he stared at the white lines in front of him when a military convoy passed him going in the opposite direction. Suddenly it hit him where Jack was headed. He remembered Jack said most of Tesla's papers were being held at Wright-Patterson Air Force base. *That's where the son of a bitch is going*, thought Wayne. *How in the hell is he going to get in there? That place is a fortress.* Wayne was deep in thought when he turned into his driveway two hours later. He pulled in his garage and stepped into the kitchen to find Betty sitting at the kitchen table with her arms crossed and wearing a resting bitch face.

"Hi honey, sorry that took a little longer than I expected."

"How'd it go in the office?"

"Oh, okay. Just some routine paperwork."

"Uh huh. And how come when I called there they said you had come and left already."

"I just had a little investigative work to do."

97

"And did this investigative work have anything to do with your friend Jack?"

Wayne looked down at the newspaper. "What if it did? What's wrong with me tryin' to get a little somethin' more for our family? I'm not ever gonna get rich as a cop, and I'm tired of workin' so hard for so little. This is a once in a lifetime opportunity. And I stumbled onto it, and I'm not gonna let it go. Jack promised me."

"That last network marketing company you were in was supposed to be a sure thing, and you lost money on that deal. We've still got boxes of stuff in our garage from that company. When are you gonna stop dreaming?"

"Never!" yelled Wayne as he stormed out of the kitchen and retreated to his office.

"And how, exactly are you supposed to make money off something that gives away free energy? Free is free. Did you think about that? Oh, never mind. You'll do what you want anyway no matter what I say. I don't know why I bother talking to you."

Wayne sat down in his chair and stared at his computer. It had never occurred to him about how you could make money by giving something away for free. He typed in Wright-Patterson Air Force Base to get an idea of what Jack was up against. *Why would he do this? I thought he was going to sell his free energy device to the highest bidder? It makes no sense going to an air base.* Wayne read that the National Museum of the USAF was housed there along with the 88th Air Base Wing. Looking at his calendar, he realized he had some vacation days. He had no idea when Jack would be there, so it was a crapshoot to go there hoping he would find him. Wayne continued his online search until the wee hours looking for anything leading him back to Cullen.

8

Jack, Ann and Arpad pored over the Tesla papers which were sprawled out over the bed in their hotel room. They had not left the room for two days gleaning over everything about Tesla technology.

"Hey, listen to this Tesla quote," said Ann. "He says if you want to find the secrets of the universe, think in terms of energy, frequency and vibration."

"That is correct," said Arpad. "Everything vibrates at its own frequency. Tesla understood that when he invented this," Arpad said as he pulled out a small black object about the size of an iPhone.

"What is that?" asked Ann.

"This is a resonator built by Tesla. As far as I know, it's the only one in the world."

"He made that himself? That's amazing! What does it do?" she asked.

"It is an electrical device that sends out signals until it matches the vibrational frequency of the object it is attached to."

"And what happens when those frequencies match," asked Jack.

"You remember the old commercials where the opera singer hits the right note and makes a wine glass shatter? Well, this does the same thing on any object it is placed on."

"Have you ever tested it?" asked Jack.

"Once, but I had to turn it off before the building came down. I placed it on my barn years ago to see what would happen. After a few minutes the old barn began to rumble, boards creaked and moaned, and the horses inside started acting crazy. I didn't want to lose my barn or my horses, so I turned it off. I had no idea if the damn thing would work or not, and I'm sure if I'd let it stay on there much longer the whole barn would have caved in."

"I haven't seen a mention of this resonator in any of the Tesla papers here," said Ann.

"That's not unusual. He conceived of inventions in his head while instructing his assistant to make a prototype for him. Tesla spoke of putting one of these on a building in New York that was under construction. He said the building started swaying and construction workers panicked and evacuated, thinking it was an earthquake."

"Did the building collapse?" asked Ann.

"No. Tesla turned it off before anything happened. There's another great story about a vibrating platform in Tesla's laboratory. Mark Twain was a friend of Tesla's and was a frequent visitor to his lab. People liked to stand on the platform while it vibrated, but it had an embarrassing consequence. The intense shaking from the platform caused an immediate need to evacuate one's bowels, and the poor unsuspecting victims would run as fast they could to the bathroom. Well, the same thing happened to Mark Twain. Tesla warned him of the consequences, but Twain paid it no mind. Twain found the vibrations pleasurable at first, but a frantic look appeared on his face after a few minutes when he realized what was happening. Twain barely made it to the bathroom in time."

"You're making this stuff up," said Ann.

"No I'm not. Look it up," said Arpad. "There's another famous story about a vibrating platform that Tesla activated one day in his laboratory. It started to shake every single building on the block to the extent that everyone was convinced it was an earthquake. The police department building was on the same block, and when it started to shake violently, they all thought it was an earthquake at first, until the police chief yelled,

"Tesla, it's gotta be him." They ran as fast as they could to his lab to see what he was up to. Meanwhile, Tesla was frantically trying to stop the vibrating platform from taking down his whole building, so he took an ax and destroyed the platform just as the police entered his lab. Tesla was convinced that within another minute his entire lab would have been destroyed."

"Arpad, what other Tesla toys do you have in that little bag of yours?" asked Ann. "We're gonna need everything you got. I know the perimeter security of Wright-Patterson is tight, so we have to create a diversion. By the way, tell me again why we're breaking into a U.S. Air Force Base with over five thousand personnel?"

"I have a few other things that I haven't shown you yet. I will show you when the time is right. Jack doesn't even know everything I have."

"Didn't you lose everything in that house fire?" asked Ann.

"No, not everything. I have a secret place for some other valuables. I can't go back to the house now because the police will question me about the body they found."

"What body?" asked Ann with a confused look on her face. "I didn't know anyone died in that fire."

"He didn't die in the fire. It was one of the goons that was following us. One of the guys that you had sicced on us," said Arpad.

"I didn't know they sent someone to kill you! I swear I didn't," said Ann as tears welled up in her eyes.

"I'm not so sure. How do we know you are not reporting back to them now? Maybe you get some kind of big fat bonus if they find us."

"Hey, come on, Arpad," said Jack. "If she was going to turn us in, don't you think she would've done it already?"

"Maybe she is waiting for the right moment," said Arpad as he glared in Ann's direction.

"Okay, Arpad. Yea, I'm gonna turn you all in right now. That's really smart. I've been out of touch with them for two days, and they are getting suspicious. I'm supposed to call them every day with your whereabouts. They are probably coming after me now, so stop your damn questions. You guys need to decide right here and now if you trust me. I'm going to take a walk so you guys can talk this through," said Ann as she got up and walked to the door.

"Whoa, there Ann. Give me your phone first," said Arpad.

Ann pulled her phone out of her pocket and slung it across the room. "There, you old fart. Check my call history yourself. You'll see I haven't made a call in two days, and my passcode is 9763." Ann slammed the door on her way out, shaking the entire room.

"Look Arpad, she's right. She would have turned us

in already. We have to trust her. We're going to need all the help we can get."

Arpad walked across the room and picked up Ann's cell phone, punched in her code and looked at her call history.

"There have been no calls for two days, but you know she could have deleted them," said Arpad.

"True. But I've got a good feeling about her. She really wants to help us."

"You better be right. We've got too much at stake to be wrong about this."

The door opened quickly as Ann barreled into the room.

"I think we're being watched."

Jack and Arpad froze. "Why do you think that?" asked Jack.

"There is a black car in the far corner of the lot with a man sitting in it. He tried to slink down in his seat when I neared his car. His skin appeared darker, like Middle Eastern maybe."

"Okay, trust her now?" asked Jack as he peered through the curtains.

"Did you call them?" asked Arpad.

"No, I gave you my phone. You could see I've called no one. I'm in as much danger as you right now. He's obviously seen me hanging with you guys, so why would I do that when I was trying to spy on you?"

"That car has been here since yesterday," said Arpad.

"We should check out and see if he follows us," said Jack. "I don't wanna be here another night. He could have called in reinforcements and is just waiting for them to arrive. Let's pack up now."

Arpad packed his Tesla devices while Jack and Ann gathered up their belongings. Arpad kept a watchful eye through the curtains on the dark car across the parking lot.

"No movement from him yet," said Arpad. "Okay, I'll go to the front office and check out. Ann, you and Jack go get the car. Unfortunately, Ann, you're going to have to leave your car. We can't split up now."

"I understand. I'm ready."

"Good. Meet me in front of the office," said Arpad.

Ann and Jack walked across the lot to Jack's car, surreptitiously watching the dark car in the far corner. Ann kept her gaze down as she put her suitcase in the trunk while Jack slid behind the wheel. He pulled to the front of the hotel, parked and spotted a dark-skinned man look in their direction as Arpad walked out of the hotel office and got into the back seat.

"Okay, don't look back at the car. I'm gonna watch him to see if he follows us," said Jack.

He pulled out of the parking lot keeping a close eye

in his mirror. After traveling a short way, Jack saw the dark car pull out and turn in their direction.

"Okay, he's behind us. What do we do now?" asked Jack.

"We can't call the police, and if we speed away, then they might stop us. We can't take the chance of explaining these Tesla toys. We'll never see them again. Let's just drive for a while and see if he follows us," said Arpad.

Jack turned right onto the interstate and watched the dark car turn and continue following him. His heart raced as he tried to stay calm and determine his next move. Suddenly, glass exploded into the car from the rear windshield.

"Get down! He just fired at us!" yelled Jack as he swerved across two lanes of traffic. Their car narrowly missed the rear of a red pickup truck in the far left lane. The dark car fired another round at Jack's car.

"Arpad, get your laser ready!

"Don't worry. I've got him in my sights now."

Arpad aimed the laser pen at the dark car's front tire melting it instantly. The dark skinned man's car slowed down and started swerving in his lane as he attempted to keep control. Jack sped up to ninety miles an hour while Ann turned around and saw their attacker pull off the road and stop on the shoulder. She drew a big breath and relaxed back into her seat.

"Nice job, Arpad," said Jack.

"I didn't want to kill him since he may have wrecked his car and hurt someone else. There's no way he can find us now unless he put some kind of tracking device on our car."

Jack glanced at Arpad and caught Ann's wide eyes in the rear view mirror, and he turned his blinker on to take the next exit. Pulling into the first gas station, Jack got out to look under the front wheel wells. He saw nothing, but Ann yelled out from the rear of the car.

"Hey, I found something, guys!" Jack and Arpad walked to the back of the car to find Ann with her head under the rear bumper. She crawled out and held up a small black box.

"This GPS was held by magnets near the right rear wheel," said Ann.

Jack examined it and handed it to Arpad, who walked over to an unoccupied white van parked at the next gas pump. After looking around, Arpad dropped a pen on the ground near the rear wheel well and placed the GPS tracker under the van.

"That should confuse him for a while," Arpad told Jack as he retrieved the pen and placed it back in his shirt pocket.

"We need to get back on the road before that guy changes his spare tire and catches up to us," said Jack.

"Yeah, let's get the hell outta here," said Ann. "Where do we go from here?"

"We've got to keep heading west towards Wright-Patterson. Let's get back on the road and then we'll figure out where we spend the night," said Jack.

"I kinda feel like a nomad now," said Ann.

"Hell, my house burned up," said Arpad. "I'm truly a nomad. Speaking of my house, I better call my insurance company. They are probably wondering where I am."

"You mean you haven't reported the fire at all?" asked Ann.

"I've been a little busy, what with people trying to kill me and figuring out how to break into a major US military base. I also need to call Magda."

"Are you nervous about seeing her?" asked Ann.

"Wouldn't you be?"

"Yeah. But I'd be excited, too. Maybe this could be the start of something for you. You said she is a widow now, right?"

"Yes. But I'm too old for that stuff."

"You crazy man, you're never too old for love."

"I've spent the better part of my life carrying the torch for Tesla and hoping to reveal his secrets this government has been hiding away since 1943. Magda can help me do that. But that is all I expect from her. Nothing more."

"You're just afraid to get hurt again, that's all," said Ann. "I can tell you still have feelings for her."

"Even if I did, they're buried too deep. Let's leave it at that."

Jack drove west on Interstate 376 as the sun began to fade. He could see the lights from Pittsburgh in the horizon, and Ann and Arpad both were sleeping when he pulled up to a Best Western with a half-lit vacancy sign. Ann woke up and looked around at the hotel surrounded by fast food restaurants and check cashing stores.

"Nothing but the best, huh?" said Ann.

"It ain't the Ritz Carlton, but it'll do," said Jack. "Let's check in and get something to eat."

9

A hundred miles away in Pennsylvania, news reports came in about the arrest of a Saudi national named Muzumdar with links to terrorist groups. Police arrested him after stopping to assist his disabled car on Interstate 376. He was found carrying an unregistered concealed weapon. During his arraignment bail was denied, and he stated he could not afford his own attorney and was sent to a holding cell to await his public defender appointment.

Amir Muzumdar spoke little during his interrogation and never asked for a lawyer after being read his Miranda rights. FBI agent Richard Bodie was fluent in Arabic but was frustrated with his lack of progress with the suspect. He left the interrogation room to speak with his boss.

"What the hell are we gonna do with this guy? He's not saying a damn thing. We've checked his visa, and it expired six months ago. His name is a match on our terrorist list from Saudi Arabia, but they have no record of any suspicious activities over there. He's been in the states for twelve years and emigrated here just before 9/11. He has no concealed weapons permit in New York where he lives. He got a flat on the side of the road and became belligerent with police when they questioned him. That's about all I have so far. You want a crack at him?"

Special Agent Sam Williams had been with the FBI for thirty-one years and was looking forward to an early retirement. He scratched his cheek, placed his hands behind his bald head and leaned back in his chair.

"Why was this guy driving on the interstate away from New York? Did he have any kind of business to attend to? How about family in the area? I wanna know why he was where he was. A motorist called 911 when he heard gunshots being fired in this area yesterday. Do you think he may have had anything to do with that?"

"I don't know," shrugged agent Bodie.

"Does he speak English?"

"I don't know. I only spoke to him in Arabic."

"You stay here. I'm going in myself to talk to this guy."

Special Agent Williams looked through the one-way

glass to the interrogation room at his suspect and started sizing him up. His subject was slouching in his seat with his arms folded and eyes cast down, so he knew he had his work cut out for him. He entered the room with a file folder and took a seat across the table from the suspect.

"So, Mr. Muzumdar, did I pronounce that right?" Stone silence followed.

"Okay, I'll go with that. I'm special agent Williams. Would you like something to drink? I have a bottle of water here."

"Yes, please."

"So, you do speak English after all," said Williams after handing over the water. Muzumdar gulped down the entire bottle in a few seconds.

"I just have a few questions for you. What kind of work do you do?"

"I'm an engineer."

"Oh really? For whom?"

"An oil company."

"Which one?"

"I'd rather not say now, as I'm afraid of losing my job."

"And you think you're going to work tomorrow, huh? You ain't goin' nowhere until you answer a few questions."

"I want to speak to a lawyer."

"Okay. You talk to your lawyer. You better tell him a

good story 'cause I got some questions for you," said agent Williams as he left the room. He came back a few minutes later with a list of attorneys and tossed it on the table in front of Muzumdar.

"Here. Pick one. Or am I assuming you can't afford your own?"

Muzumdar grabbed the papers, glaring at agent Williams.

"Let us know who you would like to speak to," said Williams as he left the room.

Pat Diradour sat in his basement office of the Pittsburgh public defender's office surrounded by unopened stacks of case files. He sipped on a diet Coke and munched on an energy bar while staring into his computer. His hair was still wet from walking in the rain from the bus stop since his 1996 Mazda was in the shop again. The phone rang on his desk, and Diradour pushed away a stack of files to answer it.

"Got a case for you," said his boss. "A man being held downtown is being charged with resisting arrest and can't afford a lawyer."

"What the hell? He doesn't need me for that. I've already got twenty cases I haven't cracked open yet, and you want me to go represent a guy for resisting arrest? Come on!"

"Oh, there's more. The feds are in on this. The guy's name has shown up on a potential terrorist list."

"Did you talk to the agent?"

"Briefly. I told him someone would get back to him."

"I'm swamped. There's no way I can take another case."

"Well, everyone else is gone, and you're the only one here, so this is your lucky day. And you're not the only one who's busy around here. Just call the station and they'll put you through."

"Thanks. Just what I needed today. A terrorist. Great. Hey, do you mind if I borrow your car to go see this guy? Mine's in the shop."

"Again? You've got to get rid of that car, Pat. How many miles do you have on it?"

"Two-hundred ninety-thousand."

"Good grief. Nobody drives a car that long. Okay, just promise you'll take care of it."

"You know I will. I'll come get the keys. Thanks."

Pat hopped in his boss's car and headed for the downtown police station still fuming over having to take yet another case. Traffic was heavier than usual going downtown, and he practiced his breathing technique his therapist taught him to remain calm. Pat noticed a stain on his tie and wished he was driving his own car since he carried a spare one in his glove box.

"Hi, Pat," said the officer at the front desk. "You've been here a lot lately."

"Yeah, too bad they don't pay me by the number of

clients. I need to go back to speak to a detainee named Amir Muzumdar. The feds are speaking to him."

"Third floor. I think you should move your office here to save you the trip."

"What? Then I'd have to see your ugly face every day. No thanks."

"Have a nice day Mr. Diradour," said the officer smiling as he buzzed the door open.

Pat knew these hallways well and took the elevator to the third floor. As he approached the entrance to the interrogation room, he noticed two men in suits he had never seen before.

"Excuse me, I'm looking for Amir Muzumdar," he said, addressing the two men.

"Are you his lawyer?"

"I might be. I'm with the public defender's office. My name is Pat Diradour."

"He's in there," said agent Williams pointing through the one way glass window into the interrogation room.

Pat peered through the window and took a deep breath. He had an unsettling feeling he didn't normally have when meeting a client for the first time.

"Hi, Mr. Muzumdar. I'm Pat Diradour with the public defender's office," said Pat as he reached his hand out for a shake. Muzumdar did not oblige and kept his arms folded.

"Uh, okay. You don't have to like me. But, believe it or not, I am here to help you. You've got the feds in here now. Do you know that is not good for you at all? Do you also know that your name has turned up on a list of those with suspected ties to terrorism?" Muzumdar sat motionless. "Did you know that?" Still no response. "Well, you better start talking or I'm walking," said Pat as he stood across the table and made a feint towards the door.

"Sit down, Mr. Diradour. I have something important to tell you."

Pat sat down across from Muzumdar and pulled a yellow legal pad out of his briefcase. He felt his client's cold, dark eyes pierce through him from across the table, and he tried to conceal his shaking hands by fumbling with his pen.

"Besides the fact that you resisted arrest, what else can you tell me?"

"Your government needs to know that its way of life is threatened by the revelation of certain technologies invented by Nikola Tesla. Many of these inventions have military capabilities and could get in the hands of the wrong people."

"Now that's the most creative excuse I've ever heard for resisting arrest. 'Yes, our government is in danger, your honor, and that's why my client resisted arrest, had an unregistered weapon and showed up on a terrorist list.' If this technology is so dangerous, then someone on a terrorist list like you would want it. So you are arguing against yourself. Got anything better?"

Muzumdar leaned forward in his chair and stared his steely eyes into Pat's.

"I am telling you the truth."

"Well, I don't know how I'm supposed to sell that cockamamie story to a judge. Why were you carrying an unregistered gun?"

"For protection."

"Well, you're in trouble for that, but you have no criminal record. How about resisting arrest? The officer said you became belligerent when he questioned you?"

"That's a lie. I never became belligerent. I just asked him several times if I was being profiled because I'm Arabic. Then he handcuffed me and I started protesting. That's all."

"Okay, I can explain that one away. But this last issue of showing up on a terrorist list is a big problem. Why would your name show up there?"

"I have relatives in Saudi Arabia that I email, and I did visit there in 2008. But I am no terrorist."

"How long did you stay in Saudi Arabia?"

"About a month."

"That's good. That's not enough time to get trained as a terrorist. But what's up with this talk about Tesla and a danger to our government."

"There's a man named Arpad Bosnyak who possesses this information. He is on the run with another man and a woman named Ann Lastrapes."

"I'm going to write these names down, but I'm not sure what relevance they have. How did you get these names, or did you just make them up?"

"I didn't make them up."

"Then tell me some more about how our government is in danger. And don't be sending me on any wild goose chases either."

Muzumdar stroked his beard and spoke softly. "Just as oil is important to the security of the United States, it is important to other countries as well. These people I have named are going to disrupt the economies of many countries with the knowledge they have."

"And what knowledge is that?"

"The ability to generate unlimited amounts of energy without the use of fossil fuels. And these people I named I believe have papers from Nikola Tesla that provide that information. My company cannot allow that to happen."

"Geez, that sounds like a helluva good idea to me. I don't see a problem there. Listen, the only problem you need to worry about is getting your skinny little ass outa here, and you ain't doin' it without a good lawyer. This conspiracy stuff is not going to go well with the judge.

He will ask you for what proof you have. Do you have any?"

"Just my contact from my company."

"Who is your company, anyway?"

"I can't tell you."

"Well, you're gonna have to tell in order to justify why you can't afford your own lawyer. They verify your employment and income to see if you can't pay. So you better tell me now."

"I'd rather pay in cash than reveal my source. Is that okay with you?"

"Alright, but if you're paying cash, then I can't defend you. I only represent people who can't pay."

"Would a fifty-thousand dollar retainer help make your decision easier?

"Absolutely. You didn't have it on you when you got arrested, did you?"

"No, but I can have someone deliver it to you. Just give me your address and I'll take care of getting it to you."

Pat handed him his card and the two shook hands. "I think this will be the start of a wonderful relationship," said Pat.

"Just make sure you get me outta here."

"You got it," said Pat as he grabbed his legal pad and headed out the door. He passed Agent Williams leaning against his doorway.

"Are you his lawyer?" asked agent Williams.

"Yes sir, I am. I'll be back tomorrow after I get a chance to read over his statement."

"You know, I really hate lawyers that defend terrorists. I know everyone is supposed to have a lawyer, but this guy is up to no good, and I don't like him. And I don't like you, either."

"Good, then the feeling is mutual. Have a good day," said Pat smiling as the elevator door closed.

Agent Williams walked back to the window with agent Bodie and peered through at Muzumdar.

"He knows something, and we're gonna beat it outta him if we have to."

10

Magda drove into Wright-Patterson Air Force Base and showed her ID badge to the security guard at the gate as she had done for over thirty years. Smiling at the guard, she tried to conceal her shaking hands. As the guard waved her on like he always did, she breathed easier. She was fully aware that stealing classified information from a government military facility could get her charged with treason. But today was the day she was going to steal every bit of information on Tesla's work that she could get her hands on.

Magda's heart had tugged at the sound of Arpad's voice the previous night. She felt like a different person speaking to him when she explained how she was going to pull her caper off. She was confident that no one would ever suspect her of anything because she had been there so long and was trusted. There was a meeting scheduled at two o'clock for some of the big brass, and Magda knew exactly where she was going to go. With only another week left on the job, she was going to give Arpad everything she could.

She entered her building which was beside one of a number of large hangars with restricted access. The base was always careful to keep all hangar doors closed to protect its contents. After scanning her ID badge, she walked down the hall to her office. Her desk was tidy and sat just outside her boss's office.

"Good morning, Magda," said Commander Dwight McKernon as she arrived right on time at 8:00 a.m. He made it a point to always beat her in to work, so she gave up trying to arrive before him years ago.

"Good morning, Commander," said Magda.

"You're so close to your retirement day. Are you excited?"

"Well, yes and no. I'm looking forward to doing some traveling, but on the other hand, I've been working here so long I'm hoping I don't get bored."

"Oh, I talk to a lot of retired people who say they are busier now than when they were working. You can do what you wanna do when you wanna do it. I can't wait to retire," said McKernon."

"We'll see."

"Trust me, you'll love it. I've got a meeting now and should be done by lunch. The only thing that you should call me about in the meantime is if a terrorist breaks in here."

"Gotcha," said Magda smiling as he walked off to his meeting.

Magda waited until the coast was clear and picked up the keys and headed to the storage room where she knew most of the Tesla papers were stored. No one had been in there for a while, so she felt safe going in as she turned on the lights. Magda practiced in her head what to say if someone walked in on her. Rows of horizontal filing cabinets lined all four walls of the storage room in alphabetical order. Her eyes picked out the letter 'T' on the front of a cabinet along the rear wall. She walked over and bent down to open the drawer. Leafing through the files she came upon a thick stack of Tesla papers crammed into the drawer which were all marked "classified" in capital red letters. *Is this how they treat sensitive information?*

Magda knew there was no way she could possibly carry all of the Tesla papers out in one day in the bag she had brought with her. She scanned one file folder of documents dated Jan. 15, 1906 that dealt with the capture and transmission of electricity wirelessly. The pages were filled with diagrams, patent references, and pictures of the huge transmitting tower Tesla built on

Long Island. Another file referenced alien transmissions Tesla received while he operated a lab in Colorado Springs.

Magda heard the sound of hurried footsteps in the hall coming toward the door, so she quickly stuffed the file in her bag and closed the cabinet drawer. Trembling, she scrambled to a corner of the room and knelt down out of sight. *What am I going to say? Is this how my career ends?* The light wasn't turned on when she came in the room, but there was no time to get up and turn it off now. As she crouched in the corner, she heard no voices, just the sound of shoes hitting the hard tile floor. Whoever was outside in the hallway was in a big hurry. Magda closed her eyes and held her breath as the feet approached the door. *This is it.* But the shoes passed by the door and continued down the hall at the same fast pace. Not daring to move, she continued listening until the sounds disappeared. Then, she cracked open her eyes, breathed deeply, and stood up to finish her job.

She found two more large files marked Tesla and pulled them out while resisting the temptation to examine them. Her heart could not take another scare like the one she just had. She glanced around the room to make sure she had not dropped anything, picked up her bag, and turned the light out. After locking the door, Magda tried to appear calm as she walked back to her office. Her insides were turning flips and her heart was racing, but she remembered to take slow deep breaths. On the way back to her office, she spotted an acquaintance approaching her from the opposite end of the hall. She prayed this co-worker would not want to stop and talk, so she picked up her pace, nodding and saying "hello," but avoiding eye contact. The acquaintance noticed her hurried steps and smiled as the two passed each other. She made it back to the safety of her office and shoved the bag under her desk. Her hands shook as she pulled out her cell phone to text Arpad.

Got them. A few seconds later Arpad responded.

Wonderful! Can't wait to read them!

Magda deleted these texts and put her phone in her purse. Her palms felt sweaty as she entered her password on her computer. With her boss in a meeting and no pressing emails to attend to, Magda turned and stared at a painting on the wall she had placed there over twenty years earlier. She had gotten so used to it being there that she had forgotten why she had bought it in the first place. Her husband was alive when she first saw it in an artist's shop, and memories of him flooded her mind. The painting was of a lone white dove perched high on a maple tree limb covered with brilliant orange-red leaves. The white dove stood out against the backdrop of colored leaves, and Magda basked in its beauty.

Then her thoughts returned to the Tesla papers in

her bag and what would happen to her if she were caught. How could they suspect her if she had retired? The end of her day and her career here could not come soon enough.

At 4:30 p.m. her boss returned from his meeting, and Magda made herself look busy on her computer.

"How was the meeting?" she asked without looking up.

"Oh, boring as usual. They announced a reorganization which won't come into play until next month, and you'll be long gone by then. When is your last day again?"

"This Friday, in two days. Hey, I know it's before five, but would you mind if I take off now?"

"Heck no, Magda. There's not much going on, so please go. You've been here, what, only thirty years? You don't have to ask. See you tomorrow."

"Thanks. I'll just go in a few minutes," said Magda as she stepped past the commander and headed to the restroom. She waited for several minutes until she felt McKernon had retreated to his office since she didn't want him to see her carrying a large bag. Magda stepped back into her office to find it empty and grabbed her purse and bag. On her way out the door, she almost bumped into McKernon returning from the restroom.

"Oh, I'm sorry. I thought you had left. Is that a new bag? I've never seen you carry that one."

"It's not brand new, but I just have a few personal effects I'm taking with me. Don't worry, I'm not stealing anything!"

"Ha! That's a good one. Enjoy your evening and I'll see you tomorrow."

"Okay. See you tomorrow."

Magda felt like she was going to pass out as she stepped into the parking lot. *Are people looking at me funny? Why are they staring at me?* She placed the bag in the back of her trunk, and as she started the car, she saw a security guard walking towards her. Magda had never been approached by any security personnel in her entire career. Her heart felt like it was going to explode in her chest. Magda rolled down her window for the guard who was now standing outside her driver's window.

"Can I help you?" Magda asked.

"Yes, it's routine now for random bag searches, and I noticed you put a bag in your trunk. Would you mind if I inspected it, please?"

"Go right ahead," said Magda, feigning indifference. "I'll open it for you."

Magda reached down and pulled the trunk latch while the young guard walked to the back of her car. Magda held her breath and watched him from her side mirror as he pulled out her bag and inspected it. *Am I being singled out? Why is he inspecting my bag?* After what seemed like an eternity, the young guard shut the trunk and walked up to her window.

"Thank you, ma'am. You are free to go."

Magda smiled and waved to the guard as she pulled out of her parking space. She pulled out her cell phone and called Arpad as soon as she had left sight of the base. Arpad was watching television in his hotel room when his cell phone rang.

"Hello, Magda. Mission accomplished?"

"Yes, but not without a scare. They searched my bag just like you said they would. Your idea of putting an identical second bag in my trunk was brilliant."

"So you hid your first bag under your spare tire compartment?"

"Yes. I just opened the cover for the spare tire and dropped the bag under it. I would have been caught if you hadn't told me to do that."

"They know that people leaving employment there are more likely to steal information. I'm sure it was routine and you are not being singled out."

"I hope so. I'm not sure if I can do this again."

"This is our only chance. There has to be information stored on a hard drive somewhere. We need to meet tonight to look at what you have so far. Can you come to our hotel? We are only about thirty miles outside of Dayton."

"Okay. Just text me the address."

"I can't wait to see you," said Arpad.

"I bet you really mean you can't wait to see the Tesla papers."

"I can't wait to see the papers and you."

Magda drove home, changed into a pretty blue dress and dabbed her neck with perfume, dancing around the house to some of her favorite music. She had not dated at all since her husband died. Taking one last look in the mirror, she hoped Arpad would like what he saw. Then she input the address on her GPS and headed east out of Dayton.

Arpad shaved for the first time in a month and frantically looked for a clean shirt in his suitcase. He pulled out his last unsoiled shirt, and to his dismay found it to be wrinkled.

"Where is the iron?" he asked Jack.

"A little nervous, huh?"

"No, just tell me where the damn iron is. This shirt is wrinkled all to hell."

"There should be one in the closet." Jack reached up and pulled an iron off the top shelf. "This must be a pretty special lady for you to get this worked up about it."

"Just shut up. Okay? I don't need you giving me crap."

"Wow. Okay. I'll lay off. I can't wait to see what she brings."

"That is the whole reason she is coming here."

"I don't believe that for a second. But I'll agree just so you don't go overboard."

Arpad took out a rickety ironing board from the closet and fumbled with it while waiting for the iron to heat up. After watching him curse under his breath, Jack bent over and opened the ironing board.

"I see that smug look on your face, young man. I don't need your help to iron my shirt."

Arpad laid his shirt on the ironing board and started to iron when they heard a knock on the door. Arpad ran the steaming iron into his left pinky and screamed in pain.

"Dammit, I hate ironing. Can you see who it is?" asked Arpad as he ran cold water over his finger.

"Who is it?" asked Jack.

"It's Ann."

"You're just in time to watch Arpad freak out," said Jack as he opened the door.

"So, Magda is on the way?" asked Ann.

"Yup. Should be here any minute. Arpad may need a little help ironing."

"I'm done here, thank you," said Arpad while putting on his freshly pressed shirt. "We need to be focused on what Magda is bringing over here about Tesla. These papers have never been seen outside of a military base before. This is historic stuff we are going to see with our own eyes."

"I can't believe it," said Ann. "I'm so excited!" The sound of three hard knocks on the door startled all of them, and they each froze and looked at each other not knowing who would open the door.

"I'll get it," said Arpad as he made his way to the door. He grabbed the handle and swung it open to reveal the one person who could still give him butterflies. The sun was setting behind the door giving an ethereal appearance to the person standing there. Magda smiled at Arpad and felt the hairs on her arms stand on end as she admired her old love. There was a brief moment of silence as the energy in the room shifted and the fading sunlight cast its warm beams on two old lovers.

"Hello, Arpad," said Magda.

Arpad stared at the beautiful woman in a blue dress standing in front of him, unable to speak. Magda dropped her black shoulder bag and stepped into the room towards him. She gazed into his eyes and eagerly embraced him. He closed his eyes and felt the softness of her body and the soaked in the smell of her hair. Memories of their time together flooded back into his mind as his defenses collapsed and tears flowed down his cheek. He remembered what it was like to be in love again and not have to speak a word. Only feel. He became aware of the others in the room and pulled back. Magda brushed a tear away from his cheek.

"Everyone, this is Magda."

"We kinda figured," said Jack. "Nice to meet you. I'm Jack."

"Hello, Jack. I've heard a lot about you."

"All good I hope."

"Yes, of course. Without you, none of us would be here. You have the original Tesla papers."

"I just got lucky."

"Hello, I'm Ann," said Ann extending her hand. "We're so excited to meet you and see what you have to show us."

"And I can't wait to see what's in this bag, too. I really haven't looked through it yet," said Magda.

"Let me grab the bag for you," said Arpad smiling. "You haven't changed a bit."

"Oh, you're a liar. Thirty years does take a toll on you. You've held up well."

"I try. Can I get you something to drink?"

"That would be lovely. It was a very stressful day. I've never stolen classified documents before. And that security guard scared me to death. Good thing Arpad prepared me for that possibility," she said addressing everyone in the room.

"Better to be prepared," said Arpad. "We have some red wine in the refrigerator. Do you still drink merlot?"

"Of course. I'm impressed you remembered after all these years."

"I haven't been able to drink merlot since I saw you last because it reminded me of you. I apologize for the plastic glasses. It's all we have. Jack and Ann, would you like some wine?"

"Maybe later," said Jack. "I want to keep a clear head."

"Me too," said Ann.

"Well, let's not keep the suspense up any more. Shall we start?" asked Magda.

"Certainly," said Arpad. "Please have a seat."

Magda reached down and pulled out three large files marked in red with the words Tesla Papers. The first file she opened was stamped classified in bold red letters at the top, and the heading was "Capture and Transmission of Wireless Electricity."

"I will read this for you," said Magda. Jack and Arpad sat on the edge of the bed to listen while Ann pulled up a chair across from her.

The electrical inventor Nikola Tesla invented a Coil for Electro magnets in 1893 and received approval via patent #512,340. This coil uses two wires laid next to each other and connected at one end. Tesla explains that this double coil will store a much greater amount of energy than a conventional coil. Like the process of liquefying air such as performed by Dr. Karl Linde, Tesla sees this device as being able to condense the energy trapped between the earth and its upper atmosphere and turn it into electricity. Here are quotes from Tesla's writings at the time of his patent: "The sun is an immense ball of positively charged electricity while the Earth is charged with negative electricity. The electrical force between these two bodies makes up cosmic rays which vary from day to night but is ever present."

In an interview with the Philadelphia Public Ledger of Nov. 2, 1933, Tesla is asked about the introduction of his fuel-less generator and whether it would upset the present economic system. His response was "It is badly upset already. Now as never before was the time ripe for the development of new resources." At a press conference celebrating his 76th birthday, Tesla announced he had invented a cosmic ray motor.

In the early 1900's, Dr. Henry Moray, a Tesla admirer, invented a machine to draw energy from the frequency oscillations of empty space. Due to pressure exerted from various government entities, the patent office declined to issue the patent.

"There's your conspiracy against free energy, right there in the governments' words. The technology has been available for a hundred years, but it has been kept a secret," said Arpad.

"Wow," said Ann. "This is going to blow the roof off

the monopoly power companies. No wonder they didn't want this out."

"This still doesn't answer the question of whether there is a current working prototype," said Jack. "That's what I'd like to see."

"Let's keep reading," said Arpad.

Tesla also claimed to receive strange signals from outer space from his laboratory in Colorado Springs in 1899. He was one of the first men to experiment with electronic receiving equipment to listen to communications from outer space. Tesla believed these communications to be from aliens. While most of the public scoffed at this idea, Thomas Edison privately believed that Tesla had found the right frequency to communicate with the dead. Edison promptly started working on a "Spirit Phone" to enable communications with the spirits of the dead. Edison died before successfully bringing this invention to fruition, but Tesla continued his work with these communications from unknown origins for the rest of his life.

"I've often read about Tesla's claims of communicating with aliens, but I'd rather read this in his own words. Look further back and see if you can spot anything in his own writing," said Arpad.

Magda thumbed through several pages of commentary until she spotted a page with someone's handwriting. She showed it to Arpad who immediately recognized it as Tesla's.

"This is his writing!" said Arpad as he arched over the papers Magda was holding. Arpad started reading Tesla's handwritten words aloud.

"The sounds I am listening to every night at first appear to be human voices conversing back and forth in a language I cannot understand. I find it difficult to imagine that I am actually hearing real voices from people not of this planet. There must be a more simple explanation that has so far eluded me."

"I am hearing more phrases in these transmissions that are definitely in English, French and German. If it were not for the fact that the frequencies I am monitoring are unusable for terrestrial radio stations, I would think that I am listening to people somewhere in the world talking to each other. This cannot be the case as these signals are coming from points in the sky above the Earth."

"This is precisely why Tesla was deemed as something as a mad scientist throughout his life," said Arpad. "People thought he was crazy for making these claims of contact with aliens. But he was not alone in hearing these transmissions. I remember a Mercury flight in 1963 where Gordon Cooper's voice transmission was interrupted by a bizarre foreign language on a channel reserved for space flights. NASA has a recording of it and it sounds like a voice grunting in an unidentifiable language."

"Before we get too much farther in these papers, we need to get hold of a working prototype of this fuel-less generator," said Jack. "This should be our main goal. Do you think they have a working model at Wright-Patterson?"

"I don't know," said Arpad shrugging his shoulders. "Magda, have you ever heard of such a thing at the base?"

"No. But I know where the restricted areas are. I can't get close to them without a security clearance, and I'm not about to apply for one now."

"It is time for Tesla's secrets to come out, and we are going to give this back for the world to use," said Arpad. "The government has no right to keep it hidden from us. Tesla tried to give help to our military during World War II, and they refused to take it. Only when Tesla died did they want his technology, and that was to keep it out of the hands of our enemies."

"How in the hell are we going to break into Wright-Patterson Air Force Base?" asked Ann. "There are exactly four of us."

"We'll have a little help from my Tesla toys," said Arpad. "And I've been formulating a plan. Here it is," he said as he displayed a diagram of the base on a sheet of paper. Jack, Ann and Magda looked at each other incredulously as Arpad explained how they were going to break into Wright-Patterson.

"Impossible," said Jack. "There's no way that would work."

"Too risky," said Ann shaking her head. "It is well guarded."

Arpad looked at Magda for some kind of affirmation.

"It can work," she said. "I'll be on the inside creating a diversion. Yes, it's risky. But it's the only chance we've got." Arpad smiled at Magda and gave her a wink.

"We should vote on whether to proceed, and it has to be unanimous," said Arpad. "I know it is risky, but this is our only opportunity. Everyone here has a chance to alter the course of history for the good of mankind. How many times in your life do you have a chance to do that?" Arpad let his words sink in as he looked into the eyes of Jack and Ann. "All in favor, raise your hand."

Arpad smiled as all four of them raised their hands in unison.

"Then it is agreed. We'll discuss this more tomorrow. They are in for a surprise at Wright-Patterson."

11

Pat Diradour walked into his office and piled another stack of files on his already cluttered desk. Two old coffee cups with stains on the bottom sat near his computer, and thus began his daily search for a clean cup. He grabbed the cups and walked to the kitchen where a new paralegal heating up a biscuit in the microwave watched in amusement at Pat's frantic search.

"Just rinse those out if you can't find one," she said as the microwave timer pinged.

"I'm in a bit of a hurry," Pat said as he opened and slammed shut every cabinet door. A clean cup in his hand at last, he dropped his dirty ones in the sink. "Thank God the pot is full."

"Heard you got a terrorist case," said the paralegal.

"Yeah, I'm getting ready to read it now," said Pat as he refilled his coffee.

"You're not gonna have that one long before the feds get in here."

"I hope not. This is a very interesting case. This guy is saying some crazy things."

"Like what?"

"You know I can't openly discuss cases. That would not be ethical," said Pat.

"Since when did you get all high and mighty? I hear cases being talked about all the time in here."

"Not this one," said Pat as he walked out of the kitchen to his office. Back in his chair, he sipped his coffee and found a sliver of room to set it down amongst the piles of paper. He pulled out his cell phone and googled new Mazda car models. After a few minutes of reverie featuring a new red Mazda, Pat pulled out the file on Muzumdar and had just started reading when he received a knock on his door.

"I'm busy. Go away." Pat thought how this interruption with a closed door would never happen in a private practice and only reinforced his desire to leave the dead-end career of a public defender.

"Uh, it's Alice." She was a wily veteran of 32 years in the public defender's office and gatekeeper extraordinaire. "I think you need to open your door. Even I can't keep out the feds but for so long."

"The feds? Why are they here?"

"They didn't explain. Now open up your damn door."

Pat felt weak in the knees as he walked to his office door. Upon opening it he saw the entire doorway of his office filled with the figure of Alice. She was a large woman who still wore shoulder pads in her dresses making her look like a linebacker. He spotted two men in dark suits, one tall and one shorter standing a few feet behind Alice.

"These men asked to see you. I didn't get the feeling I had a choice."

Pat stared at the men and got the immediate sense they were feds, but they had not identified themselves as federal agents to Alice. "Please, come in gentlemen." Pat sat at his desk while the second man closed the door behind him and sat down.

"I apologize for the appearance of my desk. I'm busy defending people. Now, who are you and why did you just barge into my office?"

The shorter man spoke first. "We are here on behalf of the Defense Intelligence Agency. The DIA collects human intelligence regarding defense issues important to national security."

"May I see some identification, please?" asked Pat.

Both men produced their ID badges to Pat who looked them over and returned them.

"Now, as I was saying, we are here on behalf of the U.S. government. We understand you have a file on a Mr. Muzumdar in your possession. Is that correct?"

"Yes, I do. But you can't have them without a court order."

The taller man pulled some papers out of a file and plopped them down in front of Pat. "Here's the court order. We are also taking over custody of this man effective immediately."

Pat looked at the court order and felt his neck and face turn red hot. "You just can't come in here and take this guy away. I'm supposed to defend him."

"Not anymore," said the tall suit. "We need all of your files on Muzumdar right away. Is that his file on top of your desk?"

"No, it's not," said Pat. Sensing his new car slip away as easily as it came, he placed several other files on top of the Muzumdar file.

Both of the agents turned and exchanged a knowing smile. It was really more of a smirk, and Pat felt like he had just been kicked in the gut.

"Mr. Diradour, we can do this the easy way, or we can do this the hard way. We have placed on your desk a court order for the files on your client," said the shorter man as they both stood up together. "You need to hand them over now," he said with an outstretched hand.

Pat looked back and forth at both men who were

standing in front of his desk. Realizing that he had no choice, he reached down and pulled out the Muzumdar file and handed it to the short man with a sigh.

"Is this all the information you have in your possession?"

"Yes, it is," said Pat.

"If we find out otherwise, then you are guilty of a felony for withholding information from the U.S. Government. Good day, sir," the short man said as they headed for the door.

"Can I ask you why you are taking my client into custody?"

"It's a matter of national security, sir. Good day," said the taller man as the door closed. Pat waited for their footsteps to fade away down the hallway before pulling a drawer open on his desk. From the back he pulled out a duplicate file on Muzumdar. He wasn't sure how he was going to use it, but he felt better having one for himself. Maybe someone would pay him some money for the extra file he had. But Pat was certain that his pay day had gone out the door with the feds.

Meanwhile, the two DIA agents made their way to the downtown prison where Muzumdar was being held. They presented their court order, and the man who had tried to kill Jack Cullen four different times walked out of prison in handcuffs. Neither DIA agent said a word to Muzumdar as they escorted him from the building and placed him in the back of their black sedan. Driving through the parking lot, the tall agent finally spoke.

"Do you think you can get Cullen this time?"

"No problem," said Muzumdar. "He's as good as dead."

12

J ack fell asleep as the sun rose on their hotel room windows. Assorted papers, empty candy bar wrappers and soda cans filled the desk and floor. Ann stepped over a stack of papers to go to the bathroom. She could hear Jack snoring from the bathroom as he lay on top of the bedspread with a stack of papers on his belly.

Arpad could not believe he was sleeping beside Magda after so many years. He watched her breathe in and out for several minutes as he reminisced about their night together. He had not been with a woman for many years, and never before had he experienced lovemaking as passionate as he had just had. Should he mention what happened all those years ago? Part of him wanted to ask her, but what difference did it make now? She was here with him at last, and that's all that mattered. Together they were going to change the world with Tesla's inventions. He lay his head down on the pillow and fell into a deep sleep, but his peaceful slumber soon turned into a nightmare causing him to thrash his legs about.

"Arpad, you're having a bad dream. Wake up," said Magda as she reached out to him.

"Ahhh!!" screamed Arpad as he sat up in bed with Magda restraining him.

"It's okay, it's okay. You're here with me. You were having a bad dream. What was it about?"

Arpad wiped his eyes and forehead and looked around to make sure he was not dreaming. "I saw flashes of light surrounding me just like the ones that used to torment Tesla. There were huge thunderbolts of lightning and loud cracks and booms. You were with me and I was trying to protect you from the storm. It was awful."

"Have you had these nightmares before?"

"Not in a long time. It felt so real."

"Let it go. Let me get you some water," said Magda.

Arpad sat on the edge of the bed while Magda tousled his hair with one hand and handed him a glass of ice water.

"Thank you."

"You still get crazy bed head hair in the morning like

you used to," Magda said as she chuckled and tried to fluff his hair around.

"Nothing can tame it except a shower," said Arpad. He grabbed her by the waist, pushed her down and kissed her.

"Ahh, you crazy old man," laughed Magda. "You haven't changed a bit. You're still just a big kid."

"I've been afraid to say anything after what happened with us before. But I know how short life is, and I can't keep those old feelings to myself anymore. I've never forgotten how you made me feel. I tried my best to bury my memories of you with work and other things, but you never went away. You faded from my mind, but you always held a special place in my heart. And now, here you are. I don't believe it. Oh, this is crazy. I'm a rambling old man."

"I'm sorry for ending it the way I did," said Magda. "I was confused and didn't know what to do. And there was some pressure from my parents. They never really liked you, you know."

"No kidding?" said Arpad with a smile.

"They never thought you would amount to anything. You had some crazy ideas back then, and they wanted me to marry someone practical. Well, I did, and I had a very safe, practical marriage. Unfortunately, it was practically without love."

"And all those years I thought you didn't care

anything for me. I had no explanation and no one to ask about you. It made for a lonely life for me."

"Well you are lonely no more. Your girl is back. I love you, Arpad. I always have and always will."

Arpad gingerly kissed her and rested his head on her chest while she played with his hair. Any memory of his nightmare slowly faded away.

"I'd like to lie here forever with you, but we've still got some work to do. My last day of work is Friday, so we've only got two days to finalize our plans. Why don't you take a shower and fix that rat's nest of hair so we can keep our momentum going?"

"You were always a slave driver. Can't I lie here with you a little longer?"

"No! Get outta bed, you lazy man!" Magda placed her feet on his backside to push him out of bed. "My parents were right. You were always a dreamer."

"Okay, okay, stop pushing me," said Arpad as he rolled off the bed and stood up.

"That's why we make a perfect team," said Magda as she rolled on her stomach, put her hands under her chin and smiled at him. "Now get in the shower!" she said motioning with her hands.

Jack and Ann continued their research into the Tesla papers next door as each made notes and highlighted areas they wanted to talk to Arpad about.

"I'm reading here about Tesla's Dynamic Theory of

Gravity," said Ann. "He offered it as an alternative to Einstein's Theory of Relativity. Tesla showed that everything is electrical and the earth is a charged sphere as it moves through space. This says he tested the first electromagnetic machine that could fly 'devoid of sustaining wings, propellers or gas bags.'"

"Wow," said Jack. "Could he have invented the first flying saucer? What else do we not know? It says here that on March 13, 1895 a New York Herald reporter came across Tesla in a small café looking completely shaken after being struck by over three million volts of electricity in his lab. Let me read what Tesla said:

"I am afraid that you won't find me a pleasant companion tonight. The fact is I was almost killed today. The spark jumped three feet through the air and struck me here on the right shoulder. If my assistant had not turned off the current instantly it might have been the end of me."

"Tesla said that he was able to see the immediate past, present and future all at once during this electrical shock," said Ann. "Unfortunately he was in an electromagnetic field and unable to do anything until his assistant came to his rescue. But the coolest thing I've read has to do with his statement that there is no energy in matter other than that received from the environment. He believed you could create a wall of light by manipulating electromagnetic waves which would enable time, space, gravity and matter to be changed at will."

"I had an experience with what I would call time travel. I was underground at Wardenclyffe when I came into contact with a Tesla coil, and the next thing I know I was lying on the pavement outside the church where Tesla's state funeral was held. I have no memory of how I got there," said Jack.

"Are you sure you weren't drunk and passed out?" asked Ann. "And did you say you were at Wardenclyffe? I didn't think anybody could get in there."

"I thought you would know since you had been following me," said Jack.

"I was following Arpad at the time and you just happened to show up. I had no idea how you got there. By the way, the people who hired me have called several times but have left no messages. I don't dare answer their calls since it could pinpoint where we are."

"That's all we need is to be found out right now," said Jack. "I've got a cop that is probably looking for me now."

"Why would a cop be looking for you?"

"Because he helped me escape my attackers, and in exchange I promised him fifty-percent of any money from free electricity technology."

"How do you make any money from something that's free?" asked Ann.

"Good question. Perhaps from selling the devices, but he didn't ask. It was just the thing to get him to help me at the time because I was in real trouble. The last guy following us is part of that same group I'm sure. He's probably following some innocent schmuck down a dead end road about now thanks to the GPS Arpad planted."

Muzumdar honed in on the coordinates of his GPS device that the DIA agents had given back to him. He activated it and found the location of the vehicle with the tracking device.

"Cullen is parked right here in Pittsburgh only ten miles or so from here. It looks like a commercial district. Can you take me there now?" Muzumdar asked.

"Absolutely. I'll log in the address on my navigation system. Okay, they are at 1269 Bellevue Ave. Let's go," said the tall agent. The black sedan sped through downtown Pittsburgh passing every car and swerving over lanes. The shorter agent handed Muzumdar a pistol.

"Here, if you kill Cullen, you get a hundred-thousand. Fifty-thousand for the old man. We want to take Ann Lastrapes alive. She was working for us and has switched sides. We need to talk to her, so don't kill her. Understand?"

Muzumdar nodded his head. "Yes. I'm after Cullen. He killed my friend by running over him with a car. And the old man killed my other partner with some crazy weapon that melted his face off. He will be the second one to die."

"We can't be seen doing any shooting, so we will have to stay in the car. The government can't be implicated in any way. Call us when you are finished so we can identify the bodies. This gun cannot be traced, so don't worry about anything. We'll back you up only if we have to. Okay, we are getting close. This vehicle is parked now, so let's do a drive by first. Turn right at the light. Okay, I think I see it."

A white cargo van was parked in front of an old metal fabrication plant in a heavily industrialized section of town. They drove by slowly, saw no one in the van, and continued past the old brick building.

"That is not the same vehicle they were driving before," said Muzumdar. "Are you sure this is right?"

"Yup," said the short DIA agent. "The ping is coming straight from that van. Stop the car so we can make sure."

Just as the car stopped in front of the building, Muzumdar swung the car door open and headed straight for the van.

"What the hell is he doing?" asked the tall agent.

"I don't know. This guy's a real headache for us. He has forgotten who he works for."

Muzumdar approached the rear of the van and looked under the rear wheel well and felt around.

Finding nothing, he walked to the other side of the van. At the same time, Jim Davis, the owner of Davis Fabricating Company, walked through the lobby of his building and noticed a stranger lurking around the rear of his company van. He stepped outside to confront what he thought was another loiterer or drunk roaming his parking lot.

"Excuse me, can I help you?" Davis said from the front door.

Muzumdar had just put his hand on the GPS tracker he found on the opposite side of the car when he heard Davis' voice. He hesitated for a moment wondering how he would retrieve the unit without this man seeing it. He pulled the tracker off and stood up while placing it in his front pocket.

"What did you just pull off my van?" yelled Davis. "I'm going to call the cops."

Muzumdar pulled his pistol out of the back of his pants and fired a shot at Davis's head. The bullet struck Davis in the shoulder, and he fell back into the glass front door holding his wound.

"What the hell did he just do that for?" screamed the tall agent.

"We're in a world of shit now," said the shorter agent as Muzumdar ran over to their car. "We should leave now!"

Before the tall agent could get the car in reverse,

Muzumdar opened the rear door and dove in. The car backed up, then sped down the street, tires screeching.

"Are you crazy?" screamed the shorter agent to Muzumdar. "Why the hell did you shoot that man? You may have blown our whole mission, you dumbass."

"You are the dumbass. That was not Cullen's van. They planted the GPS on a random car, and it led us to here. We have wasted valuable time. Unless he uses his cell phone we will not be able to track him," said Muzumdar.

Meanwhile an ambulance arrived at the scene after a co-worker had called 911. Davis walked over to the ambulance driver clutching his bleeding shoulder. "It's not too bad," he said.

The paramedic helped him into the ambulance and inspected his wound. "Who shot you?"

"I have no earthly idea. But they were messing with my van and appeared to pull something out from underneath it."

"I'm sure the police will want to speak with you at the hospital. But it looks like you'll be okay. You were lucky not to have been hit in the head or chest."

"Yeah, I guess this is my lucky day," said Davis. "I need to buy a lotto ticket. Damn vagrants."

Back at the hotel Arpad and Magda joined the others to continue with their reading of the Tesla papers.

Arpad was reading aloud but stopped when he came upon a headline in one of the last sections.

"What's the matter, Arpad?" Magda asked. "What is it?"

Arpad continued reading while anticipation built in the room.

"Come on," said Jack. "Don't keep us in suspense anymore. What the hell are you reading?"

"I was afraid that he would speak of this technology. It has the power to change the world, but not for the better. He never revealed it publicly because he knew of the dangers it would pose to the world, but now here it is in his own words and drawings. I had suspected this idea would someday get out, but we must not reveal it beyond the walls of this room. Do you all understand?"

"Yes," said Ann. "We promise. But you have to tell us now. You're killing me."

"There exists standing electromagnetic waves in a thin cavity of our ionosphere called the Schumann cavity. They are related to electrical activity and are particularly active during lightning storms. The wave frequency in the Schumann cavity has been measured as resonating at approximately 8 hertz. This happens to be in the same range where alpha waves are activated in humans," said Arpad.

"So," said Jack. "Why is that significant?"

"Because alpha waves occur when we meditate or

are in REM sleep," said Ann. "And we don't know what would happen if we were subjected to those waves from the Schumann cavity."

"Exactly," said Arpad. "Tesla theorized that humans could be controlled at this frequency to do whatever someone wanted them to do. The human race would never know what hit them. It would be the beginning of the end for humanity. No one could escape these waves. We'd all be meditating robots."

"That's crazy," said Jack.

"No, it's not," said Arpad. "I've got a secret place where I have a device handed down to me from Tesla whose purpose was never explained to me. It looks like a particle beam accelerator, but I believe it was designed to tap into the Schumann cavity and send alpha waves back to earth to control the behavior of man."

Finally, Jack broke the stunned silence. "That sounds straight out of a science fiction comic book."

"I know," said Arpad. "But this is no science fiction. This could actually happen."

"What if we used that device to get into Wright-Patterson?" asked Ann. "We could only use it long enough to go in and get what we want."

"Excellent idea!" said Jack. "Then no one will get hurt including us."

"That's a terrible idea," said Arpad. "You have not thought of the ramifications of creating alpha waves simultaneously across the globe. Pilots would crash when they are trying to land a plane, surgeons would be unable to operate. There would be too many tragic consequences."

"Like world peace?" said Magda.

"Yes, but a peaceful world with someone else pulling the strings. Mankind would have no original thought. It would not be a place I would want to live. Tesla understood that too, so he never spoke of it publicly. But he did speak about the potential to change weather patterns through the ionosphere."

"How would you do that?" asked Jack.

"If you can heat up the ionosphere, then weather patterns can be affected. People thought Tesla was crazy when he mentioned this in a speech over a hundred years ago. He wanted to create a defense shield through heating the ionosphere to help avert wars."

"So where is this secret location with this beam device you mentioned?" asked Ann.

"It's near Wheeling, West Virginia. That reminds me. I need to call the insurance company back. They probably think I burned my own house down and left town. Excuse me please."

Arpad walked outside while Jack and Ann picked up the Tesla papers to continue reading. Magda sat in her chair and gazed out the window at Arpad, thinking about the incredible night they had just had together.

Meanwhile, Muzumdar interrupted the DIA agents from the back seat.

"I've got a location on the old man. He just placed a call."

"Where is he?" asked the short agent.

"About thirty miles east of Dayton, Ohio it looks like."

"Let me map that to see how long it will take us to get there," said the tall one. "Let's see, um, about three and a half hours. Let's go now."

The black sedan squealed its tires as they made a U-turn towards Dayton.

13

_____

Jack and Ann drove behind Arpad as the orange sun set in the Pittsburgh sky. Magda leaned over and tenderly scratched behind Arpad's ear.

"Oh, don't do that now. I have to drive. I'll fall dead asleep."

"I'll make sure you don't fall asleep," said Magda. "We need to get back to Wright-Patterson by Friday. I'll take tomorrow off. I'm sure they can get by without me before my last day. I'm sure they are planning something. I don't think I could act naturally tomorrow anyway since I'd be way too nervous. Please remind me why I'm doing this."

"Because you have been working for a place that has kept Tesla's secrets hidden for too long," said Arpad. "The world is ready for this. It's Tesla's time to shine now. This information is too important to hide anymore. You are the only one who can help us."

"But I'm turning my back on my co-workers. I've been there for so long, and I feel like a traitor. I'm not sure I can do this."

"Listen, no one will get hurt. At least we are not planning on it. We are taking no guns into Wright-Patterson. Only Tesla technology will be used. Our goal is for no one to get hurt."

"Well, I've seen the security there, so believe me, there will be guns blazing if there is an intrusion."

"They won't even know we are there until it's too late."

"How will we do that?" asked Magda.

"I believe there is a device we will find that uses electromagnetic waves to bend light. The person wearing it is not visible to the naked eye."

"I've never heard of such a thing. Are you sure?"

"I was shown these devices once but they were never demonstrated. I have no proof that they work, but I believe they will."

"This is how you are breaking in? You have no proof that they work when we are risking our lives here?" said Magda, raising her voice.

"Don't worry. I have a plan. We will discuss it tonight."

Magda turned to look out the window at the passing

countryside. It was now dark, and the headlights from Jack's car shone in their mirror.

"I've always been a worrier. You know that," she said.

"Have a little faith. Tesla is the only one who knew his alternating current generators would generate hydroelectric power at Niagara Falls. Everyone else hoped it would work, but Tesla knew it would. I feel the same way about this."

After a two-hour ride on Interstate 70, Arpad turned north towards the mountains. He wound around for several miles alongside farms in the countryside before turning onto a dirt road. Driving slowly down the bumpy road with Jack and Ann behind, he stopped under a huge oak tree. A full moon lit up the sky as Magda met Jack and Ann getting out of their car.

"Where the hell are we?" asked Jack.

"Outside of Wheeling, on a farm of a friend of mine," said Arpad. "I haven't been here in years, though. Follow me."

Arpad grabbed a flashlight and took hold of Magda's hand. He led her past the tree, down to a metal grate at the foot of a hill where he knelt and pulled out a key to unlock the chains on the grate.

"This looks like a tornado shelter or something," said Ann.

"That's exactly what it's supposed to look like. Except for the chain of course."

As Arpad opened the heavy metal doors, the clanking of the rusted chains caused the crickets to stop chirping. He shined his flashlight into the dark shelter revealing a short stairwell.

"Hold my flashlight for me," Arpad said handing it to Magda as he turned around to descend the steep stairs. "Okay, you can hand it back to me now." Arpad shone the flashlight on another door inside the cave-like shelter and fumbled with his keys. "I can't remember when I've been down here last."

"Do you need any help?" called Jack.

"Yeah, you can come down and hold this flashlight for me," said Arpad.

Jack walked down the stairs into the cramped musty smelling shelter. Arpad handed him the flashlight and held his keyset up to the light to find the correct key.

"Here it is, this little one," said Arpad as he turned the lock. The doors opened to reveal a space too small to stand in. A blue plastic waterproof tarp covered a large object which Arpad leaned over to unzip.

"What is that?" asked Jack as he shined the light on an unusual looking piece of equipment that resembled a laser.

"I'm not sure, but it could be the weather

manipulator that Tesla spoke of. Help me pull it out," said Arpad.

"Damn, this thing is pretty heavy. How did they get it down here?" asked Jack.

"I don't know, but it's got to come out. There is a rope over there that we can tie around it. Magda and Ann can pull while we push from below." Arpad grabbed a length of strong rope from the floor to tie it to the laser.

"You ladies ready to do a little work?" asked Arpad as he tossed up the end of the rope.

"Sure," said Ann as she grabbed it. Magda grabbed the rope in front of Ann and placed it over her shoulder for leverage.

"Looks like you've done this before," said Ann.

"I grew up on a farm. I've pulled injured cows heavier than this thing."

"Okay," said Arpad. "On the count of three, I want you to pull, then we will push up to set it up on the steps, one at a time. Think you got it?"

"We're ready," yelled Ann.

"Okay, one, two three, pull," said Arpad.

Arpad and Jack grunted as they picked up the laser to set it on the first step. "Stop. Okay, on three...one, two, three, pull."

After the fifth step, Magda felt something snap in her back. Not wanting to stop with only one step to go and Arpad possibly being crushed underneath, she decided to keep going. "One more push boys, right now," she said scowling. "Okay, one, two, three, push."

Arpad and Jack pushed with all their strength on the bottom of the laser pedestal while Ann and Magda pulled the rope one last time.

"Aaaahh," screamed Magda as she dropped the rope and fell to the ground clutching her lower back.

"Are you okay? What happened?" asked Ann.

"Just an old lady paying the price for playing tug of war."

Arpad and Jack climbed around the laser which was now on solid ground above the steps.

"Sweetie, I knew you shouldn't have done this. I'm so sorry," said Arpad.

"Don't say that. Hell, you're older than me. I'm in this up to my neck, so I might as well sacrifice my back. I think I can stand up," said Magda. Arpad helped her to her feet as she grimaced.

"Let me rub that out for you," said Arpad.

"You don't need an excuse to touch me, lover boy."

"So you two really are an item, huh," said Jack laughing.

"I think it's great," said Ann. "True love always finds a way."

"Love can be a real pain in the back, though," said Magda. "I wouldn't do this for just anybody."

"You're not picking anything up for a while," said Arpad. "Let me help you over to the car."

"Actually, it will feel better if I just lean against the car to stretch it out. I can get there on my own," said Magda as she ambled over and leaned against the car.

"There are a few more things in the storage room I saw," said Jack. "I'll go get them."

Arpad ran the flashlight over the laser device that stood about four-feet high with two large magnets surrounding a four-foot long spherical laser.

"This looks like an instrument to heat up the ionosphere and affect the weather. Tesla sent powerful currents of electricity into the sky in Colorado Springs causing tremendous lightning storms. Residents there had never seen lightning as intense as the storms that occurred while Tesla was there."

Jack had brought up two large coils about three feet long from the shelter. "Are these Tesla coils?" he asked.

"Ah, yes they are. I was wondering how we were going to power this baby. Stick both of them into the ground about three feet on each side of the laser. That will be our power source."

"From what source will these generate power?" asked Jack.

"It's everywhere. In the air, in the ground. Energy is all around us. You just have to tap into it," said Arpad. "The Tesla coils are grounded into the negatively charged earth. This laser heats up the ionosphere with intense particle beams in the positively charged atmosphere. Remember, like charges repel, opposite charges attract. This equipment is just replicating what the earth does naturally. We should see quite a show of lightning tonight. That is, if this equipment still works. We won't need to bring everything down there with us now."

Arpad bent down to examine the laser, marveling at its beauty. He moved the Tesla coils a few inches closer to the laser and thrust the pointed metal base as deeply as it would go into the ground, then pointed the laser straight up into the sky.

"Got to have a good ground here," said Arpad. "Okay, everyone. Move back while I turn this on. I don't want any errant bolts striking you."

Arpad turned on the power switch, then joined the others who were now hiding behind the large oak tree. A low hum emanated from the laser, and after a few seconds, sparks shot out from the Tesla coils. The sparks crackled and popped, and Magda huddled closer to Arpad, still supporting her back. Jack and Ann watched dumbstruck from the other side of the tree. Suddenly, an electrical current jumped from one coil to the other, while an intense white beam of light burst forth from the end of the laser penetrating the sky above them. The hum of the laser and jumping currents from the coils reminded Arpad of pictures he had seen of Tesla experimenting in his lab.

"Wow," said Jack. "This is cool. What's gonna happen now?"

"If you look in the sky, we should start to see some lightning activity starting once the ionosphere is heated and the positively charged particles are excited. How much lightning we will see, I don't know," said Arpad. "Ah, there is our first lightning!"

"Wow, that's beautiful," said Ann as the laser continued its white beam along with the hum of the coils. The lightning increased in intensity as ominous dark clouds blocked out the full moon. The storm quickly escalated to a level none of them had ever witnessed. Drops of rain started falling on their heads beneath the oak tree as a huge lightning bolt struck the ground a hundred yards from where they were standing.

"It is not safe to stand under this tree," said Arpad. "Everyone, get to the cars, now!"

Arpad helped Magda into their car as the rain turned into a deluge. Buffy barked relentlessly from the back seat.

"Poor dog hates lightning," said Arpad. "We'll have to leave her somewhere on Friday because she will go crazy."

"Buffy can stay at my house," said Magda.

Jack and Ann ducked down and jumped in their car just as a lightning bolt touched down thirty yards away.

"This is scary," said Ann as she tried to peer out of the window. "I can't believe how quickly this started up."

"It's no coincidence that this storm started when we pointed the laser," said Jack. "But we should be safe in here."

Arpad and Magda watched in amazement at the lightning show appearing before them. Every few seconds tremendous bolts of lightning struck around them, shaking the car. Rain pounded the car and fierce winds blew small branches off the oak tree that landed on their roof.

"Shouldn't you have turned the laser off before getting in the car?" asked Magda.

"Ah, shit. I knew I forgot something. I had no idea it would get this bad so fast."

Just then a large flash blinded both of them as a huge bolt of lightning struck the oak tree. The thunder was like cannon fire as Magda closed her eyes and clung to Arpad. The tree split in two pieces right down the middle and started falling straight towards their car.

"Get down!" yelled Arpad as the tree smashed the front bumper of the car. All Arpad could see out of the front window was thick branches and leaves. He opened the door, dropped to the ground and started a belly crawl to the laser to turn it off. Magda wiped the fog off the windows to peer at Arpad crawling like a baby on the ground. The beam continued to pierce the ionosphere, and Arpad felt like he was in the middle of a war zone. He had never witnessed lightning like this and wasn't sure he would make it back to the car alive as fierce lightning bolts exploded all around. Foot by foot he crawled closer to the laser until he reached out his hand to hit the power switch. The current of electricity that stretched between the two Tesla coils stopped, and the white beam disappeared from the night sky. Soon after the laser was turned off, the lightning and rain started to dissipate. Within five minutes the thunder had slowed to a feint rumble. Arpad finally found the courage to stand up, and Magda limped over to hug him.

"You are soaked from head to toe. I was so scared you would get hit by lightning."

"You were scared. I was terrified to even move. That was the most intense storm I've ever seen. How are Jack and Ann?" asked Arpad.

"I'm not sure. Let's go check."

Just then Jack's stuck his head out from his door like a field mouse poking his head out of a hole.

"Holy shit, I didn't know lightning could ever be like that. Did we do that?" asked Jack.

"I believe we did," replied Arpad.

"Man, you're soaked," said Jack. "Did you turn it off?

I couldn't see anything. But I did see the tree get hit and fall on your car bumper. That was close!"

"Yeah, too close," said Magda, who was having a difficult time standing up straight.

"I knew we would see some lightning from heating up the ionosphere, but I did not expect this. We've found our secret weapon for Wright-Patterson," said Arpad.

"You mean we're going to attack them with weather?" asked Jack.

"Absolutely. Their power systems will likely be knocked out, so we can leave the laser on longer than I did here. There was no electrical grid to knock out here, but it will be the most god-awful storm they've ever seen. They won't know what hit them."

"What am I supposed to do on the inside?" asked Magda.

"Just take cover where you can and stay inside."

"How will we enter and exit the base without being shot at?" asked Ann. "Just because there's a storm doesn't mean nobody's guarding the base."

"It won't be a problem because nobody will see us."

"And how is that?" asked Jack

"We'll be wearing invisibility suits."

"There is no such thing as an invisibility suit," said Ann.

"There is a trunk of them right down there in the shelter."

"You're kidding, right?" asked Jack.

"I don't kid. Didn't you see a crate in the back down there?"

"I'll go look now," said Jack. "Give me your flashlight." He climbed down the stairwell and shined the flashlight into the dark recesses of the shelter where, indeed, he spotted a trunk. Grabbing the handles, he pulled the four-foot long trunk up the stairs where the others were waiting.

"It's not locked," said Arpad.

"Why didn't you tell us about them before now?" asked Jack.

"Because you would have given me crazy looks like you are giving me now. Then you never would have agreed to do this, would you?"

"Probably not," said Jack as he opened the trunk to reveal two Tesla coils on top of a stack of white full body suits. "Wow, more Tesla coils. Are these the suits we're supposed to wear?"

"Hand them to me, wise guy," said Arpad. Arpad laid out four light white suits and two Tesla coils on the ground. "These suits act to bend light around them. They only work within range of these Tesla coils which have extremely powerful magnets in them. The suits are able to bend light through refraction so the person becomes invisible. There is a clear patch in front of the eyes and two small holes to breathe out of. They're not meant to be worn for long periods of time. Here, try one on."

"What size are they?" asked Jack.

"They are all one-size-fits-all. If you are invisible, what difference does it make?" asked Arpad.

"Good point," said Ann.

"Do I leave my clothes on?" asked Jack.

"Just put the damn thing on," said Arpad. "Geezus, you ask a lot of questions."

"Well, I've never done this before. I did read about an experiment the Navy supposedly did where they degaussed a ship with Tesla coils and made it disappear. Unfortunately some sailors were melted into the ship's metal and survivors were said to have gone crazy afterwards."

"You are referring to the Philadelphia Experiment," said Arpad. "That is most likely a fabrication. The Navy did have an interest in Tesla's ideas on cloaking ships via electromagnetism, but I think that story was made up by some people with good imaginations. You are perfectly safe to try this. I assure you."

"Good thing this suit is so light," said Jack as he slipped on the suit covering him from head to toe. "Otherwise I'd burn up in here. Where are the zippers?"

"There are none since they would rust. Ann, help

him tie the sash in the back like a hospital gown. I'll turn on the coils when you are done."

"You look like a doctor wearing baggy white scrubs," said Ann as she finished tying off the sash. "Good thing you're not a patient wearing this or you might go from invisible to flashing your butt. Okay, Arpad, he's ready."

"Do I need to do anything?" asked Jack. "This feels weird that I'm actually going to be invisible. Will I be able to see?"

"Of course," said Arpad. "Your vision will not be affected. The only thing affected is the light bending around you. Ann, turn the car lights on him so we can get a good look at him before he disappears."

"Okay. Then can I try it next?" asked Ann as she flipped on the lights.

"Let's see how Jack fares first. Okay, on three. You ready? Okay, 1,2,3."

Arpad turned on the two Tesla coils which began to buzz and crackle, sending bursts of electricity towards each other until the miniature lightning bolts joined together in a steady stream. Jack stood still in front of the headlights and held an arm out to see if he could watch himself disappear before his eyes. Everyone watched as a small green fog surrounded Jack and the outline of his white suit slowly faded from sight.

"Ahhhh, where did my arm go?" yelled Jack. "This is crazy. Can you see me at all? I can see you."

Arpad squinted and peered into the darkness as the green fog lifted along with any trace of Jack. "Jack, where are you?"

"I haven't moved. I can see you, but I watched my arm disappear. I don't feel any different, but yet I'm not here."

"Start walking away from us to see how far you can go away from the Tesla coils," called Arpad. Ann moved closer to where she last saw Jack to see if she could spot the grass move under his feet. Jack took a few steps away from the group into the darkness.

"Wow, I don't see him at all. Look, I can see the grass move under his feet. Did you see that, Arpad?"

"Yes, I knew this would work," Arpad said as the Tesla coils hummed in the background. "Keep walking, Jack."

"Okay. Just tell me when to stop. It's getting a little dark out here. I don't want to fall in a hole and then you'd never find me."

"Just keep talking and we'll find you," said Arpad. Magda followed Arpad and Ann, clutching her back, which had begun to tighten up.

"Will this work just as well in the daytime?" asked Jack. "It's dark out here, ya know."

"Yes, it will work in the daytime. The only thing I'm not sure about is how far away from the coils this will operate. Just keep walking and we will find out."

"Be sure to stay behind me as close as you can. I'm worried about being bitten by a snake or something and you can't find me," said Jack.

"Don't worry, we will hear you screaming," said Arpad.

"Very funny. I'm serious."

"You'll be fine. Trust me," said Arpad.

"I think I need to rest now," said Magda. "My back is stiffening up."

"I'll go back with you to the car," said Ann as she put her arm around Magda to help her as they turned back. Arpad continued shining a flashlight on the ground to check for moving grass.

Arpad and Jack continued a running dialogue until they were almost out of sight of the glow of the coils. Ann helped Magda into the car and peered into the night to spot Arpad and Jack.

"I don't see them anymore," said Ann.

"I think we've walked close to a mile now," said Arpad. "This should be enough distance for us to get into the base. Those coils are stronger than I thought they were."

"Good. I'm ready to go back," said Jack. "This suit is hot as hell. Hey, hold your hand out for a high five. I want you to feel what it's like to be hit when you don't see it coming."

"Okay, I'll hold my hand out and you slap it," said Arpad.

Jack walked over and waved his hands in front of Arpad trying to be seen. Arpad stood holding his hand out, and Jack reached out and tickled Arpad in the stomach.

"Hey, what the hell was that?" asked Arpad. "Was that you? I thought you were going to slap my hand?"

"I couldn't resist. This is the coolest thing I've ever done. I've always wanted to be invisible. Is there any danger to staying this way for too long?"

"No. The only danger is you becoming visible again in the middle of an air force base you've just broken into. Let's join Magda and Ann and discuss our strategy."

Arpad and Jack trekked back to join the ladies and discovered Magda leaning over the hood of the car with Ann behind her massaging her back.

"Feeling any better?" asked Arpad.

"No, it's getting worse, actually. I think I need a hot bath."

"I'm going to turn off the Tesla coils and hopefully Jack won't reappear."

"Har, har," said Jack. "That's not funny. Okay, I'm ready to see myself again."

The bright white current buzzed and crackled between the two Tesla coils as Arpad reached down to turn them off. The current stopped immediately after

Arpad hit the switch, and everyone kept their eyes moving to spot Jack's return. Slowly, Jack's body suit began to appear, and Jack clapped his hands together to make sure he was not injured.

"Get me outta this thing. I'm hot as hell in here," said Jack. Ann rushed over and helped untie the back.

"What does it feel like to be invisible?" asked Ann.

"Weird. Really weird. Imagine holding your hands up and not being able to see them at all. I didn't feel any different. It just plays a big trick on your mind."

"Now we know the invisibility suits work. We just have to make sure we don't venture too far from the Tesla coils. I'll show you a screen shot on my iPad of the base and where we will enter," said Arpad as he pulled the iPad out of his car.

"What's the main thing we are looking for inside?" asked Ann.

"A working model of Tesla's free energy device."

"And do we know if they actually have one?" asked Jack.

"Well, no, but we suspect it may be in Hangar B, right here," said Arpad pointing to an aerial view of Wright-Patterson Air Base. "Right Magda?"

"Yes, it could be in there, although I've never seen it. It is a highly secure area and very few people have access to it. That is why it must be in there. But something secret is definitely in there," said Magda.

"We'll park on this road here, outside the base, and I'll set up my equipment to start heating up the ionosphere. We should have a good storm brewing in less than five minutes. That will be our distraction. I can pretty much guarantee they will lose power from this storm, enabling us to bypass their security systems."

"How will we enter the building?" asked Jack. "I know we will be invisible, or at least I hope we are, but we still can't walk through a wall."

"Magda works here in this building across from Hangar B. I will start heating the ionosphere at 10 a.m. The storm will start by 10:05 a.m., and it will take Jack and Ann at least five minutes to get to Magda's building. At 10:10 a.m., Magda will open this side door to look at the storm and let them in."

"How will I know I'm letting in invisible people if I can't see them?" asked Magda.

"Ahhh, good question," said Arpad. "Just stand by the door and they'll knock three times."

"Things are never that easy," said Ann. "I know the security of that base."

"Their power will likely be out, and don't forget they are going to be distracted by the storm of the century," said Arpad.

"Okay, and let's suppose we find this free energy device, how do we get it out of there?" asked Jack.

"Good question. You will take an additional

invisibility device to place over it, and you will carry it out. It may take both of you if it's heavy."

"I'm not sure I want to do this," said Magda as everyone stared at her in disbelief.

"Why not?" asked Arpad. "You know as well as we do how the government has kept this information silent for too long. The world has a right to this. Tesla only wanted the betterment of mankind, and we can give it to them."

"It's just...I've worked there for so long. This seems like such a betrayal. What if I get caught? What if someone gets hurt or even killed? Do I really want to spend the rest of my life in jail? I do love you, Arpad. I've never been happier than these last few days with you. But I'm not sure I can pull this off."

"Yes, you can," said Arpad. "You will not get caught. We've been through this before. And even if we get caught, none of us will implicate you. They can't catch what they can't see. And this storm is going to rock their boat. I promise you, nothing is going to happen," said Arpad as he placed his hand on her shoulder.

"Okay. But I'm doing it for you. As long as nobody gets hurt. I sure hope they aren't throwing me a surprise party."

"Well if they do, you better hope it's before 10:15, because your power may be gone," said Arpad. "We will be celebrating our discoveries Friday afternoon. Magda, do you think you could go into work tomorrow and snoop around some more? You could download some files on Tesla or try to find out what's in Hangar B."

"Well, I do know where my boss keeps his password list. He has them written on a sheet of paper in his desk. Can you believe that? Top secret sites have passwords sitting around. He has no clue."

"That's good. We should pack this equipment up and check into a different hotel outside of Dayton. You never know who might be following us."

Muzumdar and the DIA agents pulled into a hotel parking lot around midnight and parked. "This is the location of where the call came from," said Muzumdar.

"Let us handle this," said the short agent as he got out of the car. "You stay in the car, got it? Don't screw this up, okay?"

The tall agent joined him and headed towards the lobby of the Best Western. A red vacancy sign shone in the window with the "n" letter burned out. An older Indian man stood behind the counter looking intently into his computer. The DIA agents approached the counter dressed in their dark suits and flashed their badges at the manager.

"We'd like to speak to the manager of this establishment, please," said the tall agent while holding up his ID.

"That is me. My name is Brijesh Patel. How may I help you?"

"We are with the DIA and are looking for some fugitives that have crossed state lines. Do you have someone staying here by the name of Arpad Bosnyak?"

"Oh my, let me check," Patel said as he typed into his computer. "We did, but they checked out earlier today."

"How about Ann Lastrapes?"

"She checked out as well."

"Was there also a Jack Cullen with them?" asked the short agent.

"Let me check...oh, he checked out, too. I seem to remember there was someone else with them. It was an older lady, I believe. She left with the older gentleman."

"Do you have her name?" asked the tall agent.

"No, it was not given. The older gentleman paid for the room. They looked like quite the couple. All cozy with each other."

"Was there anyone else with them, or were there just four in their group?" asked the short agent.

"Oh, I don't believe there was anyone else. May I ask why you are looking for them? They were very quiet here and never really came out of their rooms."

"Government business sir. Do you know if they're returning?"

"They didn't say. I'm sorry I'm not more help. They seemed like such nice people."

"They all do. Thank you for your time," said the short agent as they turned to go back to the parking lot.

"Who is the old lady?" asked the short one.

"No clue, but we'll find out," said the tall agent as they got back in the car.

"Did you find them?" asked Muzumdar. "Are they still here?"

"No. They checked out earlier today and aren't supposed to come back. There is an older lady with the old man. I believe the manager was telling us the truth because he looked into our eyes when he spoke and didn't appear nervous at all. We just have to hope they make another cell phone call."

"I'll be ready if they do," said Muzumdar. "Too bad that I gotta kill an old lady, too."

14

Officer Wayne Claiborne tossed the sheets off his legs and stared at his clock. Three a.m. and wide awake. Again. Wayne had been looking online for days for anything that could point to where Cullen was. He had a handshake deal to split any earnings, and he had always felt a handshake was as good as a contract. That is, until he met Jack Cullen. He got out of bed and headed to his office to stare at the computer some more. He had tons of resources in the police department at his disposal, but it was as if Cullen had vanished. He'd try one last shot with an old friend who worked for the Pentagon. Though they hadn't spoken in years, Wayne found his cell number and planned to call him when the sun came up. While waiting, he googled Tesla free energy devices and saw a number of entries related to it, but most of them seemed like scams to him.

At 8 a.m. Wayne began to dial his old friend at the defense department, but then stopped dialing half-way through and pondered if he should make this call. After a few minutes, he gathered his resolve and placed the call. A male voice answered after only one ring.

"Bob Brown speaking."

"Bob, Wayne Claiborne here. How's it goin'?"

"Oh my gosh, good to hear from you, man. How are you? Are you still doing the cop thing?"

"Yes, I am, believe it or not. How's the family?"

"Oh, just great. Kirsten is working part-time and the girls are growing fast. How is your family?"

"Oh, just great. I know what you mean by growing up fast. Listen, I need a favor. We've got an arson case down here that is going nowhere finding the owner, and I was wondering if you had anything you might be able to share with me on your end."

"Sure, buddy. The owner disappeared, huh. What's the name?"

"Jack Cullen."

"Spelled C U L L E N?"

"Yup. That's it."

"What's his address?"

"366 Longwood Drive, High Bridge, New Jersey.

That's not the address of the burned property. But he is a suspect."

"Got it. Is there any reason to believe the Department of Defense should have anything on this guy?"

"Yes, he may be trying to sell classified information to a foreign power."

"Well, if that's the case then the FBI needs to be involved in this. Have you contacted them?"

"Not yet. We don't have enough evidence for that yet. I just thought I would try you first."

"Okay. Give me until this afternoon and I'll check around some and call you back. Good to hear from you, Wayne."

"Yeah, good to talk to you, too. Thanks."

Wayne grabbed some coffee in time to walk his son to the bus stop. Betty had barely spoken to him for several days.

"Who was that?" Betty asked.

"Oh, that was Bob Brown. I hadn't talked to him in years."

"So, you're getting the defense department in on this, huh? Lord have mercy, you've lost your mind again. Nothin' I say is gonna change your mind, but you can walk Derrick to the bus stop for me. I've got plenty to do around here since you are too busy to do a damn thing."

"Of course, I was just about to. You ready, little buddy?"

"Yes, Daddy."

Wayne leaned over to kiss Betty goodbye but missed as she turned her cheek away at the last minute.

"Let's go, Daddy." Wayne grabbed Derrick's hand and headed down the front steps. Betty stood in the doorway watching them walk to the end of the driveway. Wayne turned around to see Betty peering out at them before closing the door.

Magda came in to work later than usual on her second-to-last-day. She avoided everyone and snuck into the restroom when she saw someone she knew coming down the hall. Upon reaching her office, she was relieved to see that her boss was gone. Magda checked his calendar and discovered that he had a meeting until noon, which gave her about two hours to snoop around. She stepped into Commander McKernon's office and opened the unlocked drawer where he kept his password list.

Sitting at her computer with the password list partially hidden in her drawer, Magda began opening the first of several high security sites. Her heart raced as she waited for the tab entitled Tesla Papers, Classified to appear. She was astounded to read the first heading: Tesla Apparatus for the Production of Unlimited Energy.

It is true! thought Magda as she read the headline above a picture of Nikola Tesla. She heard footsteps coming down the hall and clicked off the secure site. Two high ranking officers walked past her office door and continued down the hall. Magda kept her head down and waited for the sound of footsteps to fade away and clicked back on the site.

The page read: *The electrical inventor Nikola Tesla theorized that radiant energy is omnipresent and can be tapped into with the use of his Tesla coil and a simple grounding device. While his bold public predictions, such as a death ray, were met with derision initially, we have successfully produced a prototype to produce electricity with no discernible source. Due to the sensitive nature of this and the obvious consequences in the shift of power in the world with the advent of free electricity, it was deemed too disruptive an idea to release this information now. The balance of power in the Middle East would forever be altered, and entire economies that depend on oil revenues would fail, causing widespread unrest in that part of the world. Also, U.S. interests in the exploration and development of fossil fuels runs deep, and the effects on these industries from refineries to gas stations would be devastating. This technology is to be sealed until another viable alternative renewable energy is developed for widespread commercial use.*

Magda looked up from her computer and stared at

the picture on her wall her husband had given her. Her mind raced from reading the truth behind Tesla's free energy device. She couldn't wait to tell Arpad, but making a phone call now was dangerous. Looking further in the document she noticed that there was no mention of where the device was held. Magda assumed it must have been moved around within the base over the years, and she kept on reading.

Further applications of Tesla technology can apply to the manipulation of weather. While this was accomplished during Vietnam via the seeding of clouds with chemicals, Tesla's idea was to heat up the ionosphere and possibly initiate massive thunderstorms. While this has not been experimented with, here, due to the obvious ramifications to a large civilian population, this technology is being explored at a HAARP facility in Alaska.

Magda pulled out a zip drive from her purse and inserted it into the USB port of her laptop. She knew this was information that Arpad would want, so she started to save it. As soon as she began, she heard voices coming down the hall that sounded familiar. The files had already begun to save, so she couldn't pull the zip drive out yet. What if they came into her office looking for her boss? *Hurry up*, she muttered to herself as the voices now entered her office. The download was complete, and Magda froze as she stared at Commander

McKernon standing in front of her with a young airman who looked familiar.

"Magda, oh, it's great to see you! I thought you were taking the day off."

"You know I can't bear to be away from this place," Magda said as she felt her heart skip a beat as she closed her laptop. She recognized the airman as the young security guard who had searched her briefcase in her trunk the previous week.

"Hello, I'm Staff Sergeant James Johnston," the young sailor said to Magda. "I think we met last week in the parking lot. That was a routine search, I hope you understand."

"Oh, no problem at all," said Magda. "You were just doing your job in security. We appreciate that."

"Magda, you didn't have to come in today. But you are coming in tomorrow, right?"

"Yes, I'll be here. You're not planning a party or anything, are you?"

"No, no. I know you hate those things. Our meeting ended a little early, so I'm done for the day, thank goodness. How long are you working today?"

"I'll leave around lunch, if that's okay," said Magda.

"Of course. Please come back to my office, Mr. Johnston."

"Nice to see you again, ma'am," said the young airman eying her zip drive.

"Nice to see you, too. Keep up the good work."

"I will, ma'am."

Magda waited until they had walked away before removing her zip drive and stashing it in her bra.

"She's going to be so surprised," said Commander McKernon to Johnston back in his office. "Everybody's going to be at this going away party tomorrow. We're even got people coming that retired years ago. It's going to be one helluva party."

"What time does it start?" asked Johnston.

"Ten-hundred sharp."

Magda stared at her computer but didn't remember anything she read. Her heart was still racing, and she found some papers to file to look busy. The clock on the wall seemed to be moving backwards to her. It was 11:15, and she had to hold herself back from just running out of the door to her car. She jumped when she heard Commander McKernon's office door open.

"Have a good day, ma'am" said Johnston.

"You too."

Commander McKernon walked out to Magda's desk after Johnston left. "You know, this place isn't going to be the same without you."

"Oh, you'll get by without me all right."

"I'm serious. They say everybody is replaceable, but I'm not so sure about you. You sure you wanna retire?"

"Don't get all sentimental on me now. You don't

know how hard it is for me to do this," said Magda as she stood up from her desk. "I think I better go now before I start crying."

Commander McKernon approached Magda with his arms stretched wide. "We're gonna miss you," he said as he hugged her tightly. Magda closed her eyes and fought back the tears.

"You're not making this easy for me, are you?" said Magda. "I better go before I really will cry!"

"Okay, see you tomorrow, right?"

"Right." Magda grabbed her purse and walked out of the office and down the hall to the parking lot. The bright sunny day made her squint as she fumbled for her car keys.

"Excuse me, ma'am, I'm under orders to check bags and purses today," said Staff Sergeant James Johnston. Magda was startled at first to hear someone speaking to her, but she obeyed his request and handed over her purse. Johnston rummaged around in it, and finding nothing unusual, handed it back to her.

"You get a kick going through an old lady's purse, young man?"

"Just routine ma'am. We are doing this for everyone, not just you. You can never be too safe."

"I know, I know. It just seems a shame to have to do this to an old woman who is about to retire, that's all."

"I understand. You may go. Thank you for your cooperation."

Magda got in her car and saw Johnston watching her from her rear view mirror. After tomorrow, it wouldn't matter because things were going to be different at Wright-Patterson Air Force Base forever. She breathed a sigh of relief and headed towards the base exit for a quick stop at the grocery store.

Meanwhile, Arpad, Jack and Ann arrived at Magda's home near the base to go over their plans again for their assault the next day.

"What do we do if the invisibility suits don't last long enough?" asked Jack.

"Don't worry," said Arpad. "They tested well."

Ann pored over the Tesla papers hoping to find another edge they could use.

"You know, I've been reading some more about this free energy device, and if there is one, how are we going to tell people about it?" asked Ann. "The government will come hunt us down and that is the end of our quest. We just can't come out in public and announce this without repercussions."

"I'm fully aware of that," said Arpad. "I have a plan that I was going to tell you tonight when Magda returns, but I'll go ahead now. I have a connection to WikiLeaks who will broadcast everything we have discovered. That way our identities will never be known."

"How did you meet someone at WikiLeaks?" asked Ann.

"I didn't. I just emailed them."

"It's that easy?" asked Ann.

"Yes. But it's hard to meet them in person. Lots of people would love to have them killed," said Arpad. "In fact, I've already started sending them everything that we've found out so far. You know, just in case something happens to us. This information has to live on."

"You've already leaked this?" asked Jack.

"Yes, but only to WikiLeaks. They will not publish it until we tell them to. But that should be very soon," said Arpad. "By the way, have any of you heard from Magda? She should be here by now."

"No, I haven't," said Jack."

"Me neither," said Ann.

"I'm going to call her to see where she is," said Arpad as he pulled out his cell phone.

Magda was in the checkout line at the grocery store when she saw Arpad calling. "Hello, sweetie, I bet you're wondering where I am."

"Yes, you should have been here by now. Where are you?"

"I stopped by the grocery store on the way home when I ran into an old friend. I let the time slip away."

"Well, please get home soon. We don't want to stay here tonight. We should check into the hotel near the base. I'd like to leave Buffy here, if that's alright," said Arpad.

"Of course. Okay, I'll see you in a few minutes. I love you, sweetie."

"I love you, too."

Muzumdar smiled when he glanced at his computer and saw Arpad had finally placed a call. "Got him," said Muzumdar from the back seat of the car.

"Where is he?" asked the short DIA agent.

"Dayton, Ohio."

"What the hell is he doing in Dayton?" asked the tall agent.

"Who knows," said Muzumdar. "But he is about two miles from Wright-Patterson Air Force Base."

"That's it! He's got something going on at Wright-Patterson. We have to get there now. How far is it to Dayton from here?" asked the short agent.

"Let me check," said Muzumdar. "About four hours."

"Let's go," said the tall one as he turned their car towards Dayton. "Call headquarters and tell them we have an accurate lead on their location."

"How do we know they're all together?" asked the short agent.

"Trust me, they are all in this together," said Muzumdar. "You find one rat, you find more. Or as you say, birds of a feather..."

"I'll call," said the short agent as he placed a call to DIA Headquarters in Washington D.C. to report the location of Arpad's cell phone call. After a brief conversation, he hung up.

"What are our orders," said the tall agent.

"Take whatever means are necessary to obtain Tesla information including deadly force. But they want to know what they know. That means no shooting first, asking questions later, Muzumdar. Got it?"

"Yeah, I got it," mumbled Muzumdar. The memory of the death of his two comrades was still seared in his brain.

An hour later, Officer Wayne Claiborne's phone rang. "Wayne, hey, it's Bob Brown. I've done a little digging and the DIA is all over this Cullen guy now. Turns out they got a couple guys honing in on him in the Dayton, Ohio area."

"Really?" said Wayne. "What's their location?"

"963 Willow Street, Dayton."

"Okay, that's great. Any idea why they are in Dayton?"

"No, not yet. But I'll let you know if anything else comes up. And mum's the word on where you heard this. I could get in big trouble."

"No problem. Your secret is safe with me."

Wayne looked up the distance from his home to Dayton, Ohio and saw it was over eight hours. *How can*

I explain being gone on an eight hour trip to Betty? Should I tell her the truth? Wayne's hands shook as he picked up the phone to call his wife practicing his story under his breath.

"Hello," said Betty.

"...Hi, honey, uh, listen, uh, I'm going to Dayton, Ohio to investigate a case, and I'll be gone for a couple of days..."

"Does this have anything to do with finding Jack Cullen?" interrupted Betty.

"...Yes, it does. I'm not going to lie to you. Something tells me I've got to find this guy. I'm sorry I haven't been a very good husband lately. I've been ignoring you and the kids, and that's not right. I've just become so obsessed with finding Cullen that I can't focus on anything else. If I can't find him now, then I'm giving it up and moving on with my life. But I feel like I can't be a good husband and father until I resolve this. I know you don't want me to go..."

"Listen here," Betty interrupted. "I'm glad you're finally telling me the truth. Honesty is all I want. You do what you have to do. I'll take care of things here. But when you come back, I'm taking you at your word that this thing is over."

"Okay. This is it, and I mean it. Listen honey, thank you for understanding why I need this. I'm all yours when I get back."

"Just be safe and don't do anything stupid. What does your boss think of all this?"

"I'm taking a couple personal days. He doesn't know what I'm doing. I've got so many days piled up that I've never used. He doesn't mind as long as I don't take a week off. I'll call you when I get there. I love you, sweetie."

"I love you, too."

Wayne felt a huge weight off his shoulders as he emailed his boss requesting two personal days. He stopped by his locker to hang up his uniform and retrieve some spare clothes. Grabbing a bottle of water, he headed out to his car at 4:30 p.m. Wayne figured he could arrive in Dayton in around seven hours if he pushed it. He punched in the address on his phone and headed west towards Dayton.

After a couple of hours on the road, Wayne took a break to get some dinner. He couldn't forget his chance meeting with Jack and the handshake agreement they had made. At a Subway, Wayne ordered a turkey sub and sat at an outside table to admire the sunset. Having never been to Dayton before, he googled the city on his phone while he ate.

He started reading some mundane facts in Wikipedia about Dayton as he munched on his chips. One fact caused him to stop eating, and his eyes stayed glued to the screen. Dayton was the home of Wright-

Patterson Air Force base, one of the largest air base wings in the country. It housed the Air Force Research Lab and the National Air and Space Intelligence Center, which produced research and intelligence on air defense. Wayne remembered that Jack had told him that Tesla's papers were taken to Wright-Patterson after his death and were never seen again. He knew he had no way to get inside the base, but neither did Jack. *Or did he?* Either way, Wayne was going to check out the address he had and then stake out the air base. Grabbing his sandwich, he ran out to his car, convinced Jack was up to something at Wright-Patterson.

Arpad breathed a sigh of relief when Magda stepped into her home with a bag of groceries. "I'm so glad you're back. How did it go at the base today?" he asked.

"I've got a file downloaded here," said Magda reaching down into the front of her bra.

"Wow, why did you put it in there?" Arpad asked.

"Because you told me to, remember? And my purse was checked by the same young man who searched my car before. I don't think he likes me very much."

"Why should he. You're stealing information," said Jack.

"Yeah, but he doesn't know that. At least I hope he doesn't. I just can't wait for tomorrow to be over."

"Us, too," said Ann.

"Let's go over our plans for tomorrow again," said Arpad.

"Can't we wait until after dinner? I'm cooking spaghetti."

"Okay. Then this is a good time to look at that zip drive. You should have let me take it out of your bra for you," said Arpad.

"Oh, you rascal. Calm down. There it is on the counter," said Magda. Arpad smiled, picked up the drive and inserted it into his computer while everyone crowded around the screen.

"This is top secret. No one outside of the base has seen this since the government confiscated it in 1943," said Arpad.

The first page was marked CLASSIFIED in red letters:

During experiments conducted at Colorado Springs in 1899, Nikola Tesla began to receive radio signals of an unusual nature. He would later write,"Although I could not at the time decipher their meaning, it was impossible for me to think of them as having been entirely accidental. The feeling is constantly growing on me that I had been the first to hear the greeting of one planet to another. A purpose was behind these electrical signals."

Nikola Tesla invented the Teslascope to communicate with beings on other planets. This device takes in cosmic ray signals and steps them down to audio.

Speaking into one end sends out communication from the other end as a cosmic ray emitter. The only known operating Teslascope is in high security storage here at Wright-Patterson.

Multiple attempts at using the device have yielded mixed results. Technicians were unsure how to interpret the signals they were hearing. Tesla became convinced that he had received intelligent communications with aliens. He suggested that he could transmit through the earth and air great amounts of power thousands of miles and claimed he could send a message to Mars as easily as he could Chicago.

"Wow, we just got us a Teslacope!" said Arpad.

"They must not know how to use it based on their results," said Ann. "I bet we could get it to work. Any mention of how to operate it?"

"Not yet," said Arpad. "It is possible he never drew a schematic of the device, but I always wondered if the government had one. Damn, they've been communicating with aliens. What else do they have?"

"Here is another quote from Tesla on his 75th birthday," said Arpad.

"*I think that nothing can be more important than interplanetary communication. It will certainly come someday, and the certitude that there are other human beings in the universe, working, suffering, struggling, like ourselves, will produce a magic effect on mankind and will form the foundation of a universal brotherhood that will last as long as humanity itself."*

"Do you think that Tesla really communicated with aliens?" asked Ann.

"I think he believed he did," said Arpad. "The signals he received were too distinct and rapid fire to be from natural means. This contention was what cast him as a crackpot in many people's eyes. Even Edison, Tesla's nemesis, wanted to be the first to invent the "Spirit Phone" for communication with the dead after hearing of Tesla's strange radio signals. I'm not so interested in talking with the dead."

Arpad scrolled to the next page with the heading: Electrogravatic Propulsion: Summary:

Tesla never published his dynamic theory of gravity which contradicted Einstein's theory of relativity. Air Force engineers have applied high voltage electricity to propel craft at speeds currently thought impossible. It is possible to create an artificial gravity field by charging an electrical capacitor to high voltage. The flying disc distorts the gravitational field around it and rides it like a surfboard on a wave. The craft can take this gravitational hill with it in any direction or speed. Successful experimental flights began at Edwards Air Force Base in 1954.

Future space travel will undoubtedly come from propulsion from electrogravatic vehicles as opposed to rockets. *Current hysteria over the sightings of UFO's has diverted us from placing this technology in commercial use as well as the possibility of use by our enemies. Hitler came close to perfecting a flying saucer towards the end of the war but never achieved a fully working prototype. This technology is here and now. The only question is how do we release this flying machine to the world and control its access to interests hostile to our own.*

"I don't believe what I'm reading," said Arpad. "Our government has had flying saucers for years and has been hiding them."

"So people who have seen UFO's haven't been seeing alien ships, they've been seeing Air Force piloted craft flying at unheard of speeds," said Jack.

"Yes," said Arpad. "That doesn't mean there aren't aliens, but it means that thousands of people who have reported seeing strange ships aren't crazy at all. Hell, even Buzz Aldrin said he saw a UFO on his Apollo 11 mission. They were too afraid to admit what they had seen, so they kept mum about it until a few years ago."

"He was probably seeing one of our own spacecraft. Of course, the Defense Department would never admit to having flying saucers," said Jack.

"Exactly," said Arpad. "We need to get a look at those saucers. Do you think they are in Hangar B, Magda?"

"I don't know. They won't let me near the place."

"Maybe we'll just fly the damn thing out of there," said Arpad.

"Sure. Like you know how to fly a flying saucer," said Jack.

"I was a pilot in Vietnam, so if I can fly a fighter jet, I can damn sure fly a flying saucer," said Arpad.

"You've never talked much about the war, honey," said Magda.

"It's something I'd rather forget. Anybody who likes to talk about it is a liar."

"What happened to you there?" asked Ann.

"Like I said, I don't wanna talk about it," said Arpad. "Okay?"

"I'm sorry...I won't bring it up again," said Ann.

"How about I get dinner ready?" said Magda as she turned towards the kitchen.

"Thank you, sweetie, I'll continue reading," said Arpad.

Tesla felt cosmic radiation was ubiquitous and was of a much higher frequency than what we call radioactive matter. Today, this is known as zero point radiation (ZPR) which goes from higher frequencies to lower such as ultraviolet, infrared and x-rays. Tesla announced in a New York Times article on July 11, 1937 that he had developed a system for the interstellar transmission of energy. He stated that he had built and demonstrated a working model at several undisclosed locations. No working prototype was found among his belongings after his death, and it is suspected that the Russians may have obtained this prototype from Tesla.

"Wow," said Jack. "How did Tesla think of these things?"

"He believed that the only way to world peace was to share his technologies with more than one country. For example, he gave incomplete instructions for his death ray invention to different countries before World War II with the intention that they had to cooperate to put one together," said Arpad.

"I don't think that would work today," said Ann. "Nobody trusts anybody, particularly the U.S. since the revelations that we were listening to our allies' conversations. Snowden was a traitor, though."

"And you're not?" asked Jack.

"Oh, don't go there," said Ann. "You have no room to talk. I guess we're all traitors then. I'll go ahead and address the elephant in the room. Why are we doing this? Why are we risking our lives to break into an air base to steal government secrets? I've thought about it a lot, and while I admire Tesla's work, do I really want to die for it?"

"Don't you see what they're trying to do to you to keep this information quiet?" asked Arpad. "I'm sure they would kill us on the spot for revealing the secret of free energy. These people are ruthless, and to be honest,

I don't expect to live long anyway. I've lived a good long life, but I need to leave a legacy I can be proud of. I have no children, but there are millions of people all over the world living in squalor with no working electricity. What better legacy could I leave than to give free energy to the world? Tell me!"

"I couldn't have said it better," said Jack.

"It would be a wonderful legacy," said Ann. "But I'm not ready to die yet. I wanna have children one day. I wanna fall in love. I don't wanna die alone in this world," said Ann as tears flowed down her cheek.

"You're not gonna die, Ann," said Jack wiping away her tears. "You will get to do all those things you want to do. Hell, I'm scared, too. But this is the only shot we've got. I've come to terms with living underground for the rest of my life. But again, how can they catch what they can't see, heh?"

"Yeah, as long as the damn things work during the day," said Ann.

"Trust me, they will," said Arpad.

"If you all are through arguing, dinner is ready," said Magda from the kitchen.

"We were not arguing," said Arpad. "Just clearing an elephant out of the room. This smells great! Thank you for dinner."

"Well, our last supper should be a good one," said

Magda. "Lighten up, I'm just joking," she said as they all laughed.

"Speaking of jokes, I've got a good one for you," said Arpad as he took his seat. "An old Jewish man returns from his daily prayer at the Western Wall in Jerusalem. His best friend asks him, "Hey, you've prayed at the Western Wall every day for fifty years. Can I ask what you pray about?" The old man said, "I pray that one day all Christians, Muslims and Jews will come together in peace and break bread together. I pray that politicians will work for the will of the people. And I pray for everlasting world peace among all nations." "Do you think you did any good?" asked the friend. "Nah, it's just like talking to a brick wall," said the old man.

Jack almost spit his wine out upon hearing the punch line. Arpad smiled and raised his wine glass.

"Everyone, here's to our quest to bring Tesla's free energy to the world." All four raised their glasses and clinked a toast. Ann smiled and laughed with Magda while Arpad shared another joke with Jack.

"How much further to the address in Dayton?" asked Muzumdar as their black government sedan barreled down the highway towards Dayton.

"About an hour," said the short DIA agent.

"Speed it up," said Muzumdar as he admired his eight-inch switchblade.

15

Officer Claiborne checked his GPS and rubbed his eyes to stay awake. With three hours to go, he turned the music up loud. He wasn't sure if he would even see Jack or what he would say to him if he did. He knew he was on a wild goose chase, and his marriage was on the line if he didn't resolve his quest. Wayne thought of his kids and felt like turning home to see them, but he was already committed to this. Besides, their college education could be funded with the secrets he was going to own with his supposed partner. Jack Cullen. Wayne didn't know whether he would shoot him or hug him.

Arpad helped clean up in the kitchen while Jack and Ann reviewed their plans one more time. "I'm feeling butterflies in my stomach like I'm going on my first date again," said Ann.

"Yeah, me too," said Jack. "I can't believe the day is here."

"Everybody, time to get loaded up," called Arpad as he petted Buffy. "The hotel is not far from here. It is safer if we don't stay here tonight."

"Great, another seedy hotel," said Jack.

"It's not seedy," said Magda. "I checked it out."

"Goodbye girl," said Arpad as he patted Buffy. "We'll be back to get you soon. Magda, did you leave the back door propped open for her?"

"Yes, I did. She knows how to do it."

Ann headed out to Jack's car while Arpad inspected the Tesla coils. Jack and Ann got in one car and waited for Arpad and Magda to leave first.

Wait," said Magda, turning in her seat as she put her hand on Arpad's leg. She rolled down her window and took a long, wistful gaze at her house. The setting sun on the horizon behind it caused her to squint. She heard the long past sounds of her children playing ball in the yard. The sweet fragrance of her beloved rose garden tickled her nose. "Are you sure we can't stay here just tonight?" she asked.

"We can't, sweetie. It's too dangerous. We need to keep on the move."

"I...guess you're right. It's just that I don't leave my house too often anymore."

"You can come back for more things tomorrow," said

Arpad. "They won't suspect you of anything, and we'll be long gone. I'll call you when it's safe to come meet us. Who knows, maybe we can fly away together in a flying saucer."

"I'll believe that when I see it. Okay, you can go now," said Magda. "I'm through reminiscing."

Arpad pulled out of the driveway with Jack and Ann behind. Fifteen minutes later they were checking in at a renovated Ramada only two miles from Wright-Patterson. Arpad carefully covered the Tesla coils with a black tarp in the back of his car.

"Should we leave those in the car?" asked Jack.

"It would arouse suspicion if we carried these out. Somebody might see them when we pulled them out. Besides, this is a good area, so our car is safe," said Arpad.

Arpad led Magda into their hotel room, turning to face her once inside. He put his hands on her waist and pulled her close.

"I never thought I'd see you again," he said as he stroked her hair.

"I didn't either," said Magda. "Funny how things work out sometimes."

"I never thought I'd be breaking into a United States air base with you. But there's a first time for everything," said Arpad.

"And it's only happening on my retirement day. I'm

sure they are planning a retirement party. I just pray that it is in the afternoon so I don't have to go to it. It's going to be a madhouse there tomorrow."

"They can't catch what they can't see," said Arpad smiling.

Muzumdar and the two DIA agents arrived at Magda's home ten minutes after Magda and Arpad had left. They drove by the house and made a U-turn at the end of the street.

"No car in the driveway," said the short agent. "Let's park just down the street and watch."

"I don't want to watch," said Muzumdar. "They are in there and we are going to go get them!"

"Now, listen here, dumfuck. You are taking orders from us. You don't make a move without us telling you. Understand?" said the tall agent.

"Yeah, I understand," said Muzumdar as he drew out his knife and slit the throat of the short agent. Before the tall agent could draw his gun, Muzumdar grabbed his head by the hair and sliced through his neck like butter. Both men grabbed at their necks making sick gurgling sounds while copious amounts of blood spewed freely. Muzumdar calmly wiped the bloody blade on the seat and placed it back in its sleeve. He pushed their limp bodies down in the seat, got out of the car, and walked to Magda's house. No lights were visible, so he walked around the side to the back door, peered in, then stood still listening for sounds. Hearing nothing, he prepared to punch the glass out when he noticed the door propped open.

His pistol out ready to shoot the first thing that moved, he tiptoed onto the patio where Buffy was sleeping. Aware of movement near her, she barked twice before Muzumdar fired a bullet at her head and watched as she fell to the floor. Then, as he moved from room to room, he discovered that no one was home. He hurled a kitchen chair across the room.

Muzumdar ran back to the car and pushed the short agent's limp body onto his partner's lap. He felt his feet slop in the deepening river of blood on the car floor. Muzumdar drove to the back of the subdivision, parked the car, and pulled a book of matches from his pocket. He lit a match, tossed it into the fuel tank and ran. Flames erupted from the tank, and within seconds the entire car was engulfed as Muzumdar watched from the shadows.

Back in Magda's house, Muzumdar hunted for some clean clothes. His shoes left bloody red footprints across the carpet in Magda's bedroom where he opened dresser drawers searching for a change of clothes. Finding nothing but women's clothing, he found a solitary man's three-piece corduroy suit hanging in the closet. He reached out to touch the suit but remembered he was drenched in blood. Dropping his blood-soaked clothes and shoes on the bathroom floor, he hopped in the shower. Blood sprayed off his hands and arms all over the shower curtain of Magda's bathroom, and he dried off with a nice clean white towel.

Muzumdar tiptoed naked to retrieve the suit he saw in the closet and was careful not to step in any blood he had tracked in. Slipping on the suit, he found it to be two inches short and too tight to button the waist, but he decided to go with it since he couldn't find anything else for a man to wear. Magda hadn't been able to throw away her husband's suit after he died. Finding no shoes to wear, he picked up his own blood soaked shoes and socks and tossed them into the washer. The sound of his shoes thumping against the sides of the washer was drowned out by sirens from emergency vehicles that sped past Magda's house.

Muzumdar rushed to Magda's bedroom window and saw flames from the car he had lit on fire at the end of the street. One fireman rushed to the car with a fire extinguisher while two others hooked up their hose to the fire hydrant.

"Can you see if anyone is in there?" yelled a fireman who hooked up the hose.

An explosion from the engine knocked the first fireman to the ground before he could use his extinguisher, and flames now engulfed the whole car. The other two firemen started their hose and inundated the car with water. Soon the only thing remaining was a burned out frame of an unrecognizable vehicle. After the fireman used his extinguisher to put out the remaining embers, he gasped at the sight of incinerated bodies.

"Hey, there's two bodies in the front seat," he yelled. The other two fireman walked up and stood aghast at what they saw.

"Oh, my God. They didn't stand a chance. Why couldn't they get out in time?" asked one of the firemen.

A paramedic from the ambulance walked up and grimaced at the gruesome sight. "Looks like there's nothing here for me to do," he said.

Muzumdar pulled his shoes out of the washer, grabbed a washcloth and stepped to the back door past Buffy's body, carefully wiping his fingerprints off the door handle. He could see the flashing lights of the firetruck and ambulance down the street while curious neighbors milled about. No one paid attention to Muzumdar walking down the street with squishy shoes.

Officer Wayne Claiborne followed his GPS to Magda's street and slammed on his brakes to avoid hitting a man walking in the middle of the road. The dark skinned man glared at Wayne and continued past his car. Wayne's heart pounded in his chest, and he cursed under his breath at the man in the road.

Wayne saw the fire truck lights at the end of the street and drove to see what was up before going to Magda's house. His jaw dropped when he saw the incinerated remains of a car with astonished onlookers standing around.

"I'm a police officer from New York. What happened here?"

"We're not sure," said a fireman. "There are two bodies in the front seat, burnt like charcoal. We've called the police to come get an ID on the car. They should be here soon."

"Oh, no. Thanks for your hard work. I always hated working fatalities."

"Just part of the job, sir."

Wayne turned back to get into his car and thought what a bad stroke of luck it was for the police to be swarming on the very street he was going to search for Jack Cullen. He pulled out of the subdivision just as a Dayton police officer pulled into the neighborhood. Wayne decided to get something to eat at a Wendy's he saw down the road and come back when the coast was clear for his stakeout. He hung out in Wendy's until their close, then headed back to Magda's house. By now, the street was clear, so he parked across from Magda's house. After fifteen minutes of no activity, Wayne got up his courage to do a walk around. Walking silently through the side yard beneath two large willow trees, he reached the back door, his heart pounding out of his chest. *What the hell am I doing?*

Wayne turned the handle to find it was unlocked. Stepping onto the dark porch, he saw Buffy curled up in the corner with blood running into a puddle on the tile beside her. *Who the hell would kill a dog?* Wayne walked over to check to see any signs of life from Buffy. Being a dog lover, this cruelty was unimaginable to him. Then he stepped up into the dining room and listened for any noise. He knew if there was a gun in the home, the owner would probably shoot him dead, so he decided to make his presence known.

"Jack. Jack Cullen," said Wayne out loud. "This is Officer Wayne Claiborne from New York. You know, your partner in the Tesla deal. Well, I've come to remind you of my fifty-percent stake. You do remember that, don't you? And you do remember I saved your butt by taking you in from those maniacs who wanted to kill you. I'm gonna turn the light on so you can see that it's me. If you have a gun, don't shoot. Okay...one, two, three."

Wayne turned on the lights revealing bloody footprints covering the carpet from the back door into the master bedroom. He knelt down for a closer look and saw that they were fresh wet prints. The bathroom looked like someone had been murdered with blood covering the shower curtain and a bloody white towel tossed on the floor. He left through the back door, wiping his prints off the door knob with his handkerchief. He got in his car and drove down the street with his lights out.

Wayne debated whether to make an anonymous call to 911, stopping near a pay phone by a CVS. His hands shook and his sweaty fingers slid across the metallic buttons on the keypad.

"911 Emergency."

Wayne slammed the receiver down. He decided he would call them later after he had a chance to speak to Jack, so he returned to his car. Wayne yawned as he drove around looking for a place to stay, but he finally spotted a hotel not far from Wright-Patterson Air Force Base. He checked in and started walking towards his room when he saw an old man coming out of the room next door to his.

"Hello, how are you?" said the old man.

"Tired. I'm hitting the sack as soon as I can"

"Where ya' coming from?"

"New York. How about yourself?" asked Wayne.

"About an hour west of New York."

"Small world. My name's Wayne."

"Arpad. Nice to meet you. Good night."

"Good night."

Meanwhile, Muzumdar found a grove of trees not far from Wright-Patterson where he could lie down for the night. He rolled up his vest to use it for a pillow as he moved around to find smooth ground. His only possessions were a knife, a handgun and revenge.

16

Arpad smiled when he woke up at the sight of Magda sleeping beside him. He tiptoed across the room, quietly opened and shut the door, and rapped three times on Jack's door. After a short while, the door cracked open slightly, revealing a sleepy eyed Jack.

"This is the day," said Arpad. "Can we go over our list one more time?"

Jack rubbed his eyes and turned to look around when Arpad spotted Ann sleeping in the bed.

"Oh, I see you're busy..."

"Hold on," said Jack, closing the door while he reached for his clothes. He met Arpad outside, sporting a bad case of bedhead.

"You dog! I didn't see this coming," said Arpad as he smiled and punched Jack in the arm.

"Neither did I. I'm as surprised as anyone. She's afraid of what's gonna happen today. So I started talking to her to calm her down, and the next thing you know... Well, what was I supposed to do?"

"You will make a good couple," said Arpad.

"Couple? Who said anything about that? This felt like the last supper or something."

"Well, you both get dressed and we'll go down for breakfast."

Officer Claiborne turned over in his bed and was surprised to discover he had slept until 8:15 a.m. After he showered and texted his wife good morning, he left his room and walked down to get his free hotel breakfast. Grabbing a bagel and coffee, he headed out to his car to get to know the area around Wright-Patterson Air Force base well.

At 8:30 a.m. Magda walked to her car and kissed Arpad goodbye in the parking lot.

"See you in a little while," said Arpad.

"I guess I won't see you," laughed Magda.

"Everything's gonna be all right," said Arpad as he hugged her. "Wish me luck."

Magda got in her car and smiled at Arpad as she pulled off, but her smile quickly faded. *Why am I doing this? Is there going to be a party? How can this possibly work?*

She parked and was relieved to not see a throng of

people waiting for her arrival. It seemed like any other normal day going to work with people hurrying to get their day going on a military base. Walking into her office she was happy to find no balloons, cake or surprise gatherings anywhere. The dread of having her name live in infamy as a traitor hung heavy around her neck.

"Good morning, Magda," said Commander McKernon as he walked past her desk to his office.

"Good morning, sir."

"How about we have lunch together today? How does noon sound?" he asked, standing in his doorway.

"That's great," answered Magda relieved that Arpad's break-in would spoil any plans of a party.

At 9:30 a.m. Jack, Arpad and Ann climbed into Arpad's car and headed to Wright-Patterson Air Force Base. Arpad had studied Google Earth to find the most advantageous place to set up his equipment. Several rows of tall trees lined the road on the northern end of the base. The perimeter fence had a small pond inside it and was the closest point to Hangar B. Large trees would offer good cover for their car, and only two-hundred yards of open ground stood between the fence and the hangar. At 9:40 a.m. Arpad pulled into a grove of trees where everyone began unloading the Tesla coils.

"Wait as long as you can before putting on your white suit," said Arpad. "Anyone driving by would be suspicious of three people in strange white garb outside the fence of a military installation."

"And this isn't suspicious enough with these coils?" asked Jack.

"Let's pull them from the grove of trees at the last second before firing the beam up into the sky. It shouldn't take long. We have to stay on schedule."

At 9:55 a.m. Magda eyed the clock and looked out the window from Commander McKernon's office. Only a few puffy white clouds floated in the beautiful blue sky. Back at her desk, she surfed the internet for a few minutes when her boss poked his head in from the hallway.

"Magda, hey, could you come with me to the cafeteria for a second? We've got a few more retirement papers we forgot to get you to sign. Human resources asked me to bring you over."

"Oh, okay," said Magda. "I thought I had signed everything already."

"Oh, it's just tying up a few loose ends," said McKernon as they walked together down the hall. "Better to do this now than have to call you back later. Besides, I don't think you want to come back here after you retire, anyway."

"Oh, I'm sure I'll find some reason to come by," said Magda as they approached the cafeteria. She noticed the small glass windows in the doors had been covered up, and her stomach knotted up as she approached the door. McKernon stood to the side and pushed the door open which seemed to move in slow motion, revealing a packed room of over one hundred people. Yellow and red helium balloons released at once, and the music of Kool and the Gang's song Celebration Time filled the air. A huge banner was strung across the room with the words *We'll Miss You, Magda!* Spontaneous applause and shouts echoed in the room which was filled with smiling faces. The crowd closed in closer to her, and Magda felt the urge to turn and run away as her worst nightmare had just come true. She placed her hands over her mouth in horror.

"Look, everyone here loves you," said McKernon as he put his arm around her shoulder. Magda still was unable to bring herself to utter a word. "Look everyone, for the first time in her life, she is speechless," said her boss into a microphone. Magda's legs wobbled as she took a few steps, and she would have collapsed if McKernon hadn't been there to hold her up.

"Come see your cake," he said as he guided her to a table with a beautiful dark chocolate cake with *We Love You Magda* written in yellow frosting. McKernon shoved the microphone in her hands for her to speak.

"I...I don't know what to say. Wow," was all Magda could muster as everyone cheered for her again.

At exactly 10:00 a.m. Arpad fired up the Tesla coils

and directed the laser beam straight into the sky. He found a gap in the trees to aim the laser, so he was pleased that he didn't have to expose his location. Jack turned on the smaller coils to initiate the light bending invisibility suits, and he and Ann gazed up at the sky to watch the bright beam pierce the atmosphere. Nothing happened for the first two minutes, and Jack held up his hands in exasperation at Arpad who held his palms toward Jack to calm down. Suddenly, dark clouds started forming, and within minutes the sky was pitch black with threatening cumulonimbus clouds. Thunder started out as a slow rumble and built into an earth shattering thunderstorm. The howling wind blew down a branch from the trees narrowly missing Arpad who kept his hand steady on the laser. Rain fell in torrents, and Jack felt the drops sting his body like he was being shot by a million bullets at once. Arpad motioned for Jack and Ann to move to break through the fence. A green fog enveloped the three of them as they slowly disappeared.

Officer Wayne Claiborne turned on his headlights at the first sign of the developing storm. He had never seen blue skies turn so threatening in such a short amount of time. Wayne had made several trips around the perimeter of the base and hadn't seen anything unusual. The sideways blowing rain pelted his car reducing visibility to a mere ten feet, so he pulled his car over to the side of the road. Lightning crashed down every few seconds, illuminating an ominous black sky. Wayne knew he was not going to venture out into the crazy storm. Anyone caught outside was in mortal danger from flying debris or a lightning strike.

Inside the cafeteria, attention had turned from Magda to the hellish storm that had begun outside. Everyone gathered near the windows to watch the lightning spectacle.

"Where the hell did this storm come from?" asked McKernon. "There wasn't any rain in the forecast today."

Just as he spoke, a huge lightning bolt struck a lone red oak tree just outside the cafeteria. The bolt struck the top of the oak, and within seconds, one half of the tree crashed through the large glass panes of the cafeteria windows, trapping several people underneath its branches. Glass flew everywhere, and pandemonium ensued. McKernon scrambled through overturned chairs and shards of glass to try to free the people who were trapped. Driving rain and forty-mile-per hour winds blew through the gaping hole in the side of the cafeteria. The screams of everyone inside were almost as loud as the raging storm outside.

"Somebody call 911," yelled McKernon as he attempted to pull a large branch off a woman who appeared to be knocked unconscious. Magda found her way out of the madness in the cafeteria to the door Arpad had directed her to open for her invisible accomplices. As she stood by the door and peered through the window, she watched two cars slam into each other in the parking lot in the driving rainstorm.

Arpad joined Jack and Ann at the fence perimeter. All three dropped to their bellies to keep low from the lightning flashes around them. Arpad pulled out the small laser from his suit pocket and burned a hole through the bottom of the fence. The Tesla coils had successfully begun its light bending magic, and on cue each of them held hands. Ann squeezed through first on her belly followed by Jack and finally Arpad.

Sensors went off inside the main security tower at the base indicating a fence breach, and the security guard assigned to monitor the screens turned his attention to the perimeter fences. A massive lightning bolt made a direct strike to the roof of his tower knocking out all power, followed by a blackout of the rest of the base. After the backup generators failed to turn on, the guard called his superior on his emergency walkie talkie to report the news.

"Sir, this is Adams in the main tower. We are operating in the dark. Backup generators failed for some reason. We are vulnerable right now to intrusion. Suggest deploying personnel to perimeter fences."

"Negative," came the reply from his superior. "Too

dangerous with this storm. Anybody trying to get in here is crazy to be out in this shit anyway. They'll be struck by lightning before they get anywhere. I've never seen anything like this. It's like a war out there."

Arpad knew he only had about ten minutes before the effects of the storm would start to wane, and he reached out to grab the invisible hand of Ann who in turn reached out for Jack's hand. They walked together as lightning bolts exploded all around them. Ann was temporarily blinded by a lightning strike thirty feet away, so she clung to Arpad's hand as they made it to the waiting Magda. Upon hearing three knocks, Magda opened the door and felt the rain pelt her face. Standing by the open door, she was startled to feel something touch her shoulder. She didn't see anyone, but she realized it was Arpad when he squeezed her arm to let her know they were okay.

Magda followed their plan and led them to the hallway entering Hangar B. What was usually a tightly controlled access was now easily accessible with the blackout, and security personnel were left scrambling to communicate. Magda pointed them in the right direction and stepped back out of their way. Jack, Ann and Arpad were now in the restricted, high security Hangar B at Wright-Patterson Air Force Base. Arpad looked at a watch inside his suit to see they only had nine minutes left of storm cover and wondered whether he should have stayed back to continue his assault on the ionosphere with the laser. But then he remembered the prize he was after...Tesla's free energy device was probably hidden here.

He pulled on Ann's arm so hard she almost fell to the ground. The personnel in the hangar were scattered about, and Arpad, Jack and Ann walked right in front of them undetected.

Arpad stopped to check behind a closet door causing Ann to bump into him. Finding nothing, Arpad closed it and then led them to a hallway where he spotted a door at the end of the hall with a *Danger High Voltage* warning sign on it.

The hallway was dark as the power was still out, and the thunderous booms from lightning shook the walls of the hangar. Arpad led the others past some large electric panels and transformers when he saw something familiar resting in the back corner, up against the wall.

A three-foot-tall black stake with a small rectangular electronic device attached at the top reminded him of a figure he had seen in one of Tesla's drawings. Beside it was a two-foot tall Tesla coil which he grabbed and covered with an extra towel-sized piece of the invisibility suit he had brought.

Arpad also saw what appeared to be the famous Teslascope lying on the floor. Surely, this was too important to leave unsecured like this, so he picked up the bullhorn like device and shoved it inside his suit.

Power was still out when Arpad led his group out of the electrical room and back into the hallway. The storm outside still raged, but the frequency of the lightning blasts had dwindled. Arpad figured they had about five minutes before the storm faded and pulled Jack and Ann quickly behind him, carrying the hidden Tesla coil, stake and Teslascope.

They entered a smaller part of the hangar filled with workbenches. The hallway would have been pitch-black except for a single skylight that let in a sliver of light. Arpad saw nothing unusual as they crept through but stopped in his tracks when he saw a door swing open in front of him, almost striking him in the face.

An armed security guard stepped out directly in front of them and Arpad caught hold of the door before it closed. He watched the young, tall guard leave the room, allowing him to look behind the door. Jack opened it and led the others into a jet black room. Stumbling around in the dark, he finally found something to prop the door ajar so they could find their way out. Suddenly, the lights in the hangar came back on, along with the whooshing sound of the air conditioning system. Jack, Ann and Arpad couldn't believe what they saw in front of them.

Three saucer-shaped crafts sat in the room looking just like something out of a science fiction magazine.

Ann grabbed Jack's arm.

"Holy shit," said Jack.

Arpad ran to the first saucer, admiring its sleek design. It stood about twelve feet high and about twenty-five feet across on an elevated set of tripods. He ran his hands over the black ceramic tiled exterior admiring its smooth surface when he touched something that caused a set of stairs to extend down from the saucer to the floor. Barely believing his luck, he stuck his head into the opening and climbed the stairs with Ann and Jack right behind him.

A cylindrical tube ran through the middle of the craft, and a windshield wrapped around the entire machine offering a three-hundred-and-sixty-degree view. Arpad placed the coils and Teslascope behind a small compartment in the back.

"I can see both of you now," said Ann.

"I guess something about this ship negates the light bending properties. It doesn't matter because I'm gonna fly this thing right outta here," said Arpad.

"How the hell are you gonna do that?" asked Jack. "You've never flown a flying saucer before."

"No, but there's a first time for everything. Hell, if I can fly jet fighters, I can fly a damn flying saucer!"

"Well, since these suits don't work in here, can we take them off?" asked Ann.

"I say, yeah," said Jack removing his headgear. "I'm hot as hell in this thing."

"I guess it's okay since we're in here. But keep them close as we may need them again," said Arpad as he removed his suit. "We need to figure out how to fly this thing."

"But first we gotta figure out how to open that hangar door," said Jack.

"Jack, can you go try that red knob on the wall over there?"

"Sure thing. I'll be quick."

Jack bounded down the steps, slapped the knob on the wall, causing the large hangar doors to peel open.

"Awright," yelled Jack. Arpad turned his head when he detected someone standing in the doorway of the hangar. He grabbed his laser to defend himself from a trigger-happy guard, but his jaw dropped when he saw Magda standing there.

"Oh my God, what is she doing here? I guess she wanted to see this for herself," said Arpad as he stepped off the craft to meet her.

Magda smiled when she saw Arpad and started running towards him. Suddenly, the familiar face of Staff Sergeant James Johnston appeared in the doorway behind her. The guard who had searched Magda twice before raised his gun.

"Run, Magda, run!" yelled Arpad.

Johnston aimed his handgun and fired. Magda felt a sharp pain as the bullet hit her in the back and exited through her chest. She placed both hands over the gaping wound, stopped, and fell to her knees as blood spilled onto the clean hangar floor.

"Nooooo! Magda!" Arpad screamed as he raced towards her. A second shot missed Arpad who pulled out his laser and fired, striking the guard's neck and severing his head from the rest of his body. The head clunked on the floor before the body followed a few seconds later. Arpad rushed to Magda's aid.

"Sweetie, why did you come here? This was not part of the plan," said Arpad as he held her in his arms.

"I... I just had to see what was in here. And I wanted to see you, too," said Magda as she started to go into shock. Blood had now soaked her clothes deep red as her hands failed to stop the bleeding. Arpad placed his hands over her open wound.

"We'll get you to a doctor," screamed Arpad. "I'll figure out a way to get you outta here. You're gonna be okay," said Arpad as tears flowed down his cheeks.

"Did you find what you were looking for?" asked Magda. Her face grew pale as the blood continued to flow out of her body.

"Yes, we did."

Magda took one last gaze into Arpad's eyes, smiled, and died in his arms.

"No! No! No!" screamed Arpad. "God, no. Why her and not me? This is my fault. I'm sorry, honey. I'm so sorry." Arpad wailed as he continued holding on to her. Jack walked over to Arpad and put his hand on his shoulder.

"I'm so sorry. I know you loved her. But she would want you to complete your mission, and there's gonna be backup now that there's been shots fired. We've gotta get outta here. The power is back on, the storm is ending, and we aren't invisible anymore."

"I can't just leave her here," sobbed Arpad. "What am I supposed to do?" Emergency sirens started alerting the entire base of an intrusion. The lightning had ceased and the rain had slowed to a light sprinkle. Arpad sat on the floor still holding on to Magda, brushing back her hair. Jack looked up when he heard the sounds of approaching boots.

"Arpad, they're coming after us. We've gotta leave now!" yelled Jack as he drug Arpad away from Magda and helped him towards the craft. Arpad cried and turned back to look at Magda's body lying on the floor. "Don't look back," said Jack as he ushered him inside where Ann was crying. She hugged an inconsolable, shaking Arpad.

The sound of bullets striking the craft brought Arpad back into the moment.

"Get this thing off the ground now!" yelled Jack. Arpad wiped his eyes and sat down at the control chair. The control panel was simple with only one row of switches, and the entire craft only had four seats. Jack sat beside Arpad while Ann secured herself in a rear seat.

Arpad tried a few switches and found one to close the stairwell. A dozen guards were now firing from the tarmac outside the hangar. Arpad focused his old pilot skills and ran through a mental checklist as bullets ricocheted off the surface of the craft. He pulled a throttle bar up, and the craft jerked upwards almost crashing into the roof of the hangar before Arpad reversed his throttle pull only to bounce the ship off the hangar floor. Twenty more guards now joined in firing at the saucer. Arpad surveyed the panel and pushed the first button by the throttle down, catapulting the craft out of the hangar at a light speed just over the guard's heads. While sonar pulses detected obstacles and maneuvered the craft away from danger, Arpad had traveled a mile in less than a second while flying no higher than thirty feet.

"What just happened?" asked Ann from the back seat. "Where did they go?"

"That was us moving at an incredible speed, but I felt nothing," said Arpad.

"Can you get this thing off the ground now?" asked Jack. "They're gonna come after us again. How in the hell did you not run over anything just now."

"I have no idea," said Arpad. "Let me try pushing this throttle up and then hit this switch. Hang on." In an instant the craft was a thousand feet in the air.

"What the hell?" said Jack. "That's crazy. I didn't feel a thing. We should be sick from G force, but it's like nothing happened."

"Remember, Tesla wrote about an anti-gravity machine that pushes gravity away and rides it like a wave. This whole ship is shielded from gravity. That's why it can move at an incredible speed and the occupants will feel nothing," said Arpad.

"Better keep moving," said Jack as the sound of bullets hitting beneath the craft made him squirm in his seat. "I don't wanna get hit in the jewels."

Arpad pushed the throttle and the switch together, propelling them miles from the base at ten thousand feet. "Wow," said Arpad. "I don't believe how fast this is. There is no sound, only effortless instant acceleration. No wonder they wanted to keep it hidden. They let us think there were aliens flying these. But all along, it was us."

"So, all those unexplained UFO sightings over the years were real," said Ann.

"Most of them were," agreed Arpad, "but some of them probably were experimental aircraft. We need to go retrieve our coils from the ground before they are discovered."

"If they haven't been found already," said Jack. "You can bet they're sending up fighter jets after us."

"A fighter jet is of no concern to us. They can't match our speed. The technology of propulsion jets to this craft is like comparing a bow and arrow to a nuclear weapon," said Arpad. "But I'm not going to give their radar a chance to find me, so I'm going down now."

Arpad began a zigzag descent and was hovering a hundred feet above his car in a matter of seconds. "I'm not quite sure how to land this thing," he said.

"I hope you're a quick learner," said Ann. "I just spotted a fighter jet take off from the base."

"Let's see what this switch does." Arpad flicked a switch, and a bright spectrum of red and white lights illuminated the exterior. "That's not what I want," he said as he turned off the lights.

"Oh, no," said Jack. "By the way, three cars are stopped by the side of the road staring at us and taking video with their phones. We're gonna be on the news tonight!"

"Everybody, put on your invisibility suits again. No

one can know our identity," said Arpad. "Let me try this switch." When he hit the control, the craft started a slow descent as the landing gear automatically deployed, and the craft touched down on the grass beside the car. "Let's hope the Tesla coils are still operating. Okay, is everybody ready to disembark?"

"Yup," answered Jack.

"Okay, Jack, you drive the car back to Magda's house and leave it there in the driveway. Look for us at the end of the street." Arpad's voice choked when he realized he had mentioned Magda's name. "I don't know if I can ever say her name again," said Arpad with tears welling up in his eyes.

"Okay, let's gather up all our equipment and bring it back in here. I'll go in the car to retrieve all of our Tesla papers," said Arpad as he opened the stairwell hatch.

Susan Myers was a mother of three young children who had stopped her van by the road when she saw what looked like a flying saucer appear out of nowhere above her car. She had pulled out her iPhone to record the flying disc hovering above her car, and her hands shook as she videoed the ship landing.

"Oh, my, God, the doors are opening," she said while recording. "Are little green men gonna hop out now? Is this a gag or something, because this is really freaky? I don't see anyone yet, though. Wait, there's something moving...it's some piece of equipment floating in the air and moving towards the flying saucer. This is crazy. I don't believe what I'm seeing. Oh, now a door on that car just opened by itself, and now it shut. And some briefcase is floating towards the saucer. It's like somebody invisible is carrying it. I think I'm gonna pass out."

Officer Claiborne pulled up his car behind Mrs. Myers' van when he saw what looked like a flying saucer hovering in the sky. The rain had stopped, allowing a small ray of sunlight to peek through the clouds.

Jack laid the equipment back in the ship and walked back to Arpad's car. Susan Myers was unable to speak as she watched a car leave with no one in the driver's seat. Officer Claiborne followed the driverless car while keeping a safe distance back. *I bet Cullen is in on this. That has to be a Tesla flying saucer*, he thought.

"Now I've seen everything," said Susan. "Good thing I got this recorded or nobody would believe me," she said as Jack drove Arpad's car away. Arpad flew the spacecraft to Magda's house in a matter of seconds and performed a landing in a clearing at the end of the street.

Within a few minutes he spotted Jack pull into Magda's driveway. Officer Claiborne was not far behind and pulled over at the opposite end of the street from the spacecraft.

Muzumdar was watching Magda's house from across the street in a car he had stolen during the night. He slouched in his seat when he saw Arpad's car pull in the driveway. The car door opened and shut, and Muzumdar rubbed his eyes to make sure he was not hallucinating. Next he saw something strange in his rear view mirror that appeared to him to be a flying saucer, so he turned his car around to get a closer look at this strange craft.

Arpad was about to open the hatch and let down the stairs for Jack when he noticed a car approaching. The flying saucer had already grabbed the attention of an elderly woman walking her dog. Her tiny Maltese barked incessantly at the ship, and the white-haired woman was too afraid to move.

Then, Arpad recognized the man in the car as one of those who had tried to kill him at his house. With his invisibility suit intact, Arpad got off the ship and approached Muzumdar's car.

Muzumdar's eyes widened as he watched the hatch open on the ship in front of him, unaware that Arpad had walked to the rear of his car. Pulling out his resonator, Arpad bent down, attached it to the rear bumper and activated the device. Jack, still invisible, moved to a yard across the street to watch the show about to unfold.

Muzumdar felt his car begin to lightly vibrate, thinking it was just his engine knocking. After a few more seconds, his car bucked in the air like a horse and slammed back to the ground with such force that he was knocked unconscious. Arpad watched impassively as Muzumdar's car bounced around like a Mexican jumping bean. He had set the timer on the resonator to turn off after one minute, and by the end of that minute, the car looked like it had been in a demolition derby. Muzumdar's neck had been broken during the violent thrashing of his car, and he lay slumped with his car turned upside down on the pavement.

Arpad retrieved his resonator from the bumper and started walking to the craft. Officer Claiborne could not believe what he had just witnessed, but he knew that Cullen was there somewhere.

"Jack...Jack Cullen. I know you're here," yelled Wayne from down the street. Jack turned around and spotted his old friend walking in the middle of the road.

"Listen, buddy, you remember our deal, right? Fifty-fifty partners. You never told me you had a flying saucer," said Wayne laughing.

"Just tell me this," continued Wayne. "I haven't forgotten about you. Have you forgotten about me, 'cause I gotta know. If you have, that's okay. I...I just need to move on. So, if you're there...just tell me." Wayne listened through the deafening silence for several seconds, and hearing nothing, hung his head and turned back to his car.

"No, I haven't forgotten about you," yelled Jack from

the stairwell of the flying saucer with his headgear removed. They exchanged smiles before Jack waved goodbye and retreated to the ship.

"Yesssss..." said Wayne as he pumped his fist in the air.

"Let's get out of here," said Arpad as he took controls of the flying saucer. A fighter jet made a low flyover above them, but Arpad paid it no mind. Pushing the throttle, he flew a hundred miles away from Wright-Patterson Air Force base in less than one minute.

A rescue squad arrived on the street to check out reports of a wrecked car and a white-haired woman who had passed out while walking her dog.

17

Within twenty minutes Arpad had arrived outside Toronto and the home of his WikiLeaks confidant Suresh Nayyar. His home was tucked off a private road in the mountains which afforded some privacy for the landing of a flying saucer. Arpad handed him the rest of the classified documents for review and publication on WikiLeaks.

"You know, WikiLeaks does not publish everything it receives. There is a review process with final say going to Julian Assange," said Suresh.

"I understand," said Arpad. "The first thing I want to do is to test this device I picked up from Wright-Patterson Air Force Base. I want to see if it generates electricity."

"Um, that's interesting," said Suresh. "I've never seen one of those devices. This is quite exciting!"

"I'll set it up outside," said Jack.

"I'll help you," said Ann. "I can't wait to see if this really works?"

"I think Officer Claiborne would do a back flip if it does. He thinks this is his pile of gold. But let's see if this thing works."

Suresh took them beside a garden in his back yard for the experiment. Arpad thrust the three foot pole into the ground between the two Tesla coils.

"This is how I think Tesla would have placed them," said Arpad as he flipped a switch on both the coils and the middle stake. The low, gentle hum of the coils blended in harmony with a nearby waterfall flowing over moss covered boulders in the garden. Arpad stood ten feet away and held up a single light bulb in his hand. With no cords or obvious power source, the light bulb lit up in Arpad's hand.

"This is unbelievable," said Ann. "How does it work?"

"Radiant energy from the earth and sun," said Arpad. "The earth is negatively charged while the air is positively charged. Now this is just a small example with a low watt light bulb. But think of the implications across the world where there is no power at all. Billions of people can now have access to free electricity. Tesla saw it as a fundamental right just like breathing clean air. And now, the secret is finally going to get out. We can fulfill his vision. I wish Magda was here to see this."

"She's with us," said Ann as she put her arm around Arpad. "I can feel her with us now. She didn't die in vain."

"Absolutely," said Jack. "Suresh, what's the best way for us to proceed?"

"Power companies are going to fight this. They will spread a campaign of distortion and lies saying free energy devices are hoaxes and will never work on a large scale if at all. What we can do is hold them hostage by threatening to release the technology to WikiLeaks if they don't start adapting renewable energy technologies like wind and solar. I can't believe we are still burning coal for energy in the twenty-first century. They will only react if there is pressure for them to act. When they do what we want, then we release the device anyway," said Suresh.

"Right," said Arpad. This is for the world. We need to build a movement from the people to create a demand for it. People won't believe it until they see it for themselves. I have a contact in an NGO in Liberia that would love to see this. Let me send this to him. They are just getting a handle on the EBOLA virus situation there, and he will be happy to look at this. We can make this thing go viral."

"And what do we do with our little space ship?" asked Jack. "We can't hide this thing forever."

"Let's wait on that for now. I want to get Tesla's free energy idea going. Will this spacecraft fit in your barn?" asked Arpad.

"I think it will. Why don't we try it now before a drone comes by," said Suresh.

Arpad moved his space ship into the barn with plenty of room to spare. "I'm gonna miss flying this thing. I'm just getting the hang of it. It's a helluva ride."

"We need another bargaining chip with the government for renewable energy," said Suresh. "If they knew we had this, they'd kill all of us to get it back. I cannot believe you actually have a flying saucer, much less one from a U.S. air base. This is some crazy stuff, man. You guys are incredible."

"I can't wait to see the look on my friend's face in Liberia when I ship this free energy device to him," said Arpad. "We have the schematics to make more of them."

A month later a large box arrived in Monrovia, Liberia, sent to the director of a non-profit food agency. The box contained detailed instructions of how to set up the free energy device and included twelve dozen light bulbs for a demonstration. Arpad had instructed his friend to record the demonstration at night and to recruit one hundred and forty-four children for the event.

Following a beautiful yellow sunset on the beach of

Monrovia in western Africa, one hundred and forty-four excited young children were each given a light bulb to hold. Cameras were set up from several angles to record the event, and two large Tesla coils were placed into the sand in the beach with a large stake in the middle. The director of the non-profit had the children count down from ten before he hit a switch on the coils. The children ranged in ages from five to twelve and splashed their feet in the waves until the countdown was finishing. "Three, two, one..."

A camera from the roof of a nearby hotel caught the simultaneous lighting of one hundred and forty-four light bulbs on the beach. The next camera angle showed the expressions of wonder and surprise of the children as they held a bright light bulb high above their heads. They laughed and shrieked and held it up to their friends' faces.

Within two days, the video on YouTube of the free energy device in Liberia had gone viral with over thirty million views. Hundreds of videos taken from cell phones emerged of a flying saucer in Dayton, Ohio and near Toronto. Power companies worldwide put out press releases debunking the idea, calling it a hoax. OPEC countries called the video a fake, but the start of the Tesla free energy revolution had begun.

Arpad, Jack and Ann gathered to watch the video from Liberia one more time. The momentum for free energy was gaining speed, and Arpad penned a letter to the U.S. Department of Energy and to President Obama. WikiLeaks released the following statement on their website the same day:

"WikiLeaks will reveal the story of the government conspiracy to suppress the ideas of Nikola Tesla. These include the now widely distributed ideas of free energy for all and the revelation of the existence of flying crafts known to the public as flying saucers. Failure to admit this cover up will result in the release of even more sensitive documents."

Julian Assange

Jack and Ann hugged and pulled out a bottle of champagne to celebrate while Arpad hung his head.

"What's the matter?" asked Ann. "You're missing Magda, aren't you?"

"Yes, I'll never get over her. This is bittersweet because this is what Tesla wanted. I was only carrying out his wishes. You know that this is not over. This fight has just begun, and I don't have the energy to fight it anymore. The forces against this are more than you know. I wish Magda were here. I have lost more than I have gained, but I can die in peace and leave my mission to you to carry on."

"But we need you," said Jack. "We can't do this alone."

"I have started the energy revolution, my friend.

Tesla waited his whole life for this moment. My mission is complete, and I pass the torch from Tesla to you. If you will excuse me, I'm going to go for a walk."

With those words, Arpad got up and walked outside of his Canadian friends' home. The cool autumn air felt refreshing to his mind, and he looked to the western mountains where the setting sun cast an orange glow. A single dove flew overhead, and Arpad admired its graceful flight against the backdrop of green trees. The silent beauty of the mountains was interrupted by the whirring of helicopter propellers.

A startled Arpad turned to look at the helicopter as it passed in front of him. A high powered rifle emerged and fired a single shot, striking Arpad in his chest. He fell backwards, clutching his wound as the helicopter turned away.

Lying on his back, Arpad could hear his friends' screams as they ran towards him. He reflected on his life, and smiling, gazed into the blue sky filled with puffy white clouds. The lone white dove circled ten feet above him, and Arpad closed his eyes.

To those readers who are concerned about the effect that burning fossil fuels is having on our fragile environment, please support the use of renewable energies such as solar and wind, visit www.renewableenergyworld.com, or buy a Tesla like I did and enjoy the best car you've ever driven.

    – *Dan Sizemore*

ALSO BY DAN SIZEMORE

The Money Maker

A Network Marketing Adventure

My Triumph

The Misadventures of a Middle-Aged

man in a British Sports Car

Visit www.dansizemore.com

for more information

If you enjoyed the book,
please post a review.
It would be greatly appreciated.

Dan grew up the youngest of four children in the small town of South Boston, VA. His father was in the real estate and insurance business and was a renowned storyteller. His mother was a talented singer and music teacher. Dan inherited the love of storytelling from his father and followed in his father's footsteps into the insurance industry. His love of music comes from his mother who guided him into piano lessons at an early age. He loves playing the music of Billy Joel, the Beatles and Scott Joplin.

After graduating from Va. Tech, Dan moved to Richmond, Virginia where he met his future wife Carolyn. After a 17 year career in the insurance business, Dan left his insurance business when his wife got a job transfer to Jacksonville FL. He made the transition to become a stay-at-home dad for his two young children.

Dan's first book, *The Money Maker*, was inspired by his real life experience in the network marketing industry which he discovered is a great way to have people head for the hills. His first book of the trilogy *Tesla's Secret Papers* is a science fiction thriller based on some of the revolutionary ideas from the electrical genius and inventor, Nikola Tesla. His love of anything related to Tesla caused him to buy the car bearing his name.

Dan loves golf, but he completely understands why Mark Twain called the game "a good walk spoiled." His favorite musical artist is Bruce Springsteen. He's read everything written by the author Michael Lewis and is an avid investor.

Dan resides in Jacksonville, FL with his wife and is adjusting to empty nest syndrome while his two daughters attend college.

FOR MORE INFORMATION

www.dansizemore.com